Ty pulled her from the floodwaters

She stared at him then in shock as he brought down his mouth and drew gently on the thin gash oozing tiny beads of blood on her arm. "No!" Her face flushed with color.

"Antiseptic." He looked up, catching the extent of her inner turmoil. "What are you really frightened of, Morgan? Some powerful magic?"

"Frightened?" Her emerald eyes flashed. "I didn't realize you were a vampire?"

His eyes were very blue and very searing. "Maybe I hunger for a little affection."

"No, Ty," she said, "I have no tender feelings for you."

He gave an ironic smile. "So why are you panting when I touch you? Why have your eyes grown so strange and enormous?"

Morgan drew in her breath sharply as she felt the surge of some primitive emotion—something alien....

Margaret Way takes great pleasure in her work and works hard at her pleasure. She enjoys tearing off to the beach with her family on weekends, loves haunting galleries and auctions and is completely given over to French champagne ''for every possible joyous occasion.'' Her home, perched high on a hill overlooking Brisbane, Australia, is her haven. She started writing when her son was a baby, and now she finds there is no better way to spend her time.

Books by Margaret Way

RISE OF
AN EAGLE

Margaret Way

Harlequin Books

TORONTO • NEW YORK • LONDON
AMSTERDAM • PARIS • SYDNEY • HAMBURG
STOCKHOLM • ATHENS • TOKYO • MILAN

Original hardcover edition published in 1988
by Mills & Boon Limited

ISBN 0-373-03012-6

Harlequin Romance first edition October 1989

CHAPTER ONE

AT dawn of the day Edward Hartland was buried, great billowing thunder clouds like silver-shot atomic mushrooms began to roll in from the desert. To the north and the south, to the east and the west, they massed and hung in barbaric splendour, so close to the earth that some of the aborigines were wide-eyed with a sense of foreboding, and the whites on the station were forced to take deep, calming breaths to keep their own sense of proportion. Today the man who had dominated their lives for more than a half-century was being taken up into the Sky World and a peculiar dread bordering on panic throbbed in the atmosphere. Edward Hartland had not been loved. He had been revered like a stern and sometimes dangerous god.

His granddaughter, Morgan, triangular face set in planes of mourning, stood behind the lace curtains of her bedroom watching a long procession of vehicles wind up the avenue of sentinel desert oaks, a full mile from the front gates of the compound to the homestead. People, a few genuine mourners among them, had been arriving all morning. They came from all over the great State of Queensland and beyond. The Hartland empire spread its tentacles all over the continent and now they came, stout Outback vehicles lining both sides of the undulating drive and light aircraft scattered like giant birds off the all-weather strip. Professional mourners by the hundred: family, so-called close friends, politicians, rich graziers, the landed establishment, hangers-on, socialites, all of them acknowledging the passing of a legend in his own lifetime. His enemies far outnumbered his admirers and only his granddaughter, Morgan, was said to love him.

Why were you such a cold, difficult man? Morgan thought. Why was there so little loving kindness in your heart? She turned away from the window bleakly. Many a time she had suffered from his savage moments. No one had a more lashing tongue than E.J., though God knew Ty could be perfectly hateful. For someone who had been so kind to her when she was a child, she now thought of Ty as the enemy, her natural-born rival, and the hostility was mutual. She and Ty couldn't be together five minutes before the sparks flew. She even hated him enough to wish he had stayed away from the funeral, but then the whole Outback would have been shocked. All of them were E.J.'s family and subjects. It was unthinkable that his only male relative should not be there to stand at his graveside.

Now there's a boy who'd love to stand in my shoes! E.J. had often taunted him. Don't think I don't know all about your burning ambitions, young Tyson!

Ty had never answered. Never taken the bait. He had simply stood his ground, dark blond head thrown up in his damn-you-to-hell attitude, azure gaze brilliant and quietly scornful. *Who cares what you think?* the gaze said, and E.J.'s thick black brows would move down over his hooded eyes like thunder clouds. As far back as Morgan could remember, there had been a special tension between E.J. and Ty, a continuance of the long-ago rivalry between E.J. and his stepbrother, Robert. Robert had been the favoured one, causing a bitter, lifelong jealousy and resentment in the loner, E.J.

Of such things were feuds born. Morgan turned about to the long mirror. Her eyes looked strange, shadows beneath them. They were *very* green, large and tilted like a cat's, as was the triangular shape of her face. Her highly individual appearance was the cause of her name. Her mother who had given her up so easily had thought such a queer little baby should have an odd name. Morgan was a faery name and it was true that as Morgan grew she developed a wild beauty in startling contrast to the other Hartland women. Ty's sisters, Sandra and Claire, were exceptionally good-looking with haloes of golden hair and the vivid blue eyes of the Hartland clan. They didn't present the compelling front of their brother, but they were universally known as the 'beautiful Hartland twins'. Morgan's beauty was far more elusive and complex. At times with her eyes hidden, and when all was not well she could look almost plain, but then her extraordinary slanting eyes would flash up, emerald green like a still lake, and her long raven mane would curve around her face and one was certain she had power of some kind.

It's all too easy to believe you're a witch!

Woe betide you, Ty, if I were.

She looked sallow and washed out in black, and no number of tucks could disguise the fact the dress did not belong to her. Cecilia had brought it with her, but whereas the Hartland women were tall and stately, Morgan was small and slight. The dress was too big and too long, and though she had belted it very firmly around her tiny waist the effect was dismal. She just knew Cecilia and the girls would look very different. Not that she cared. Morgan was as terrible in her way as was Ty. The two of them had always had an alarming tendency towards rebellion. The only thing they had in common. The only apparent family tie. Strangers on first meeting them did not think they could conceivably be related, for somehow Morgan had inherited quite different genes.

Her mother had not come. Marcia never could face the pressure-points of life: marriage, motherhood, being left a young widow. She had hated E.J. as much as she was capable of hating anyone, so why *would* she come? Marcia had long since become the prize possession of the silver-haired, Chairman of the Board of Just About

Everything, Sir Philip Ainsley. Morgan had the black-printed telegram on her dressing-table. The problem was, Philip's commitments did not allow them to get away, but both sent their fondest love and deepest sympathy. Her mother had deserted her long ago. Morgan remembered the day vividly. Her mother had visited her at her boarding-school, sweeping her small eight-year-old daughter into her arms, resembling a mother, but never a mother, explaining in a short, private talk that Morgan's grandfather, a man of iron will, would not countenance passing his only grandchild into the care of her mother, and as his heiress Marcia would do anything to protect her little daughter's inheritance. The deal was simply that Marcia would move out of Morgan's life. Edward Hartland would assume complete control.

Morgan and Marcia had been estranged for years until Morgan, determined and challenging beneath her fragile looks, had sought out her mother on her own. She had been seventeen at the time, newly graduated from college with all the honours E.J. had expected of her. From earliest childhood Morgan had had to set her mind to gaining accomplishments. She wondered how many other twenty-year-old girls, especially twenty-year-olds of her slight physique, could ride, shoot, hunt and muster. She even had a pilot's licence, plus a sheaf of diplomas for piano, art of speech and ballet. E.J. had demanded so much of her, but however hard she tried she could never become his true heir. She could never be a boy. Though he was going to his grave without admitting it, E.J. would have thrown Morgan to the lions if he could have gained control of Ty. Ty was an identity in his own right. After his father had been killed in a light-aeroplane crash, which even now no one could satisfactorily explain, power had passed to Ty. He had taken over the reins and never looked back. For the past few years it had been a spellbinding contest between the young and old. It might have even hastened E.J.'s death to know Ty was coming out on top. Ty was a natural-born power-broker. God help her now, when he would start to cut her down to further his own ambitions. No one could deny her own flair, but she dreaded the morrow when she would be matched against Ty. Not only that, the entire clan would support him. It was a good thing E.J. had ensured her outright control.

Prior to the funeral only family were admitted to the house, though afterwards would come the inevitable gathering. Morgan walked along the quiet corridor and down the great curving stairway, and as she did so Ty came out of the drawing-room, from whence issued voices, breaking in his long stride as he looked up and saw her.

'For God's sake!' The radiant blue eyes flashed over her with their characteristic insolence. 'You might have picked out something to *fit*!'

'Keep out of my way, Ty,' Morgan advised.

'You're joking!' He was tall, lean, supple, with an animal grace of movement. He mounted the stairs in a flash, grasping her by the arm. 'Maybe you don't know it, but to everyone else all you need is a *broom*!'

'Sure,' she said. 'Don't try drinking anything I pass you.'

'Oh, my.' His vivid gaze moved to her hair. 'What the hell is that?'

'That's a chignon,' she said crisply. 'Your big problem, Ty, is you've forgotten it's a *funeral*.'

He shrugged. 'It's impossible to feel tearful. It wouldn't surprise me if the old devil tried to rise again.'

'Believe he'll be around to haunt you?'

'Not me, sweetheart.' Using his vastly superior height and strength he began to propel her back up the stairs. 'There are going to be hundreds of people here today. There's no way I'm going to let you appear looking like a joke.'

'You let me go!' she gritted, with more than a hint of violence.

'I'm not happy about what an outfit like that might do to the family. I know you're much too proud a young creature ever to have asked that miserable old miser for money, but I've seen you in a dozen outfits more suitable than that.'

'If you don't let me go,' Morgan warned very slowly and distinctly, 'I'll have you thrown out.'

At least he didn't laugh. 'Simmer down, elf,' he replied, almost mildly.

When had he last called her that? It had to be *years* ago!

Somehow they were back in her room, and while she stood in helpless rage he went to the huge armoire that held all she owned in the way of dresses and threw it open.

'My God, how pathetic!'

'Thank you. Why would I need a large wardrobe when all I wear is riding-gear?' She went to him and stared up at his arrogant profile.

'Isn't this awful? Just plain, bloody, awful.' He appeared genuinely taken aback. 'I couldn't get into either of my sister's bedrooms for the profusion of possessions. What the hell is a little girl doing in her mother's dress?'

'*This* little girl is a *woman*!' Anger was putting colour into Morgan's pallor. Her very green eyes gleamed.

'You're not even a pocket Venus. Seen from the back, I'd swear to God you were Oriental.'

'Thank you again. I think Chinese and Japanese women are just beautiful.'

'I didn't say you weren't beautiful.' He stunned her for the second time. 'God, I'm shocked,' he muttered tersely. 'It's a good thing you're such a tough little fortune cookie, otherwise I'd have to see you as a natural-born victim.'

'Get out of my wardrobe.'

He ignored her. 'What about this?' He drew out a soft grey dress on its hanger.

'I repeat,' she said tightly, 'we are going to a *funeral*.'

'You'd attract no more attention if you went in that little red bikini Pat O'Donough got so excited about.'

'Pat O'Donough is a creep.'

'I'm afraid you're right. Make him disappear so he'll never be seen again.'

'It may not work on Patrick, but it would be a pleasure to work on you.' Morgan snatched the grey dress from him, holding it to her, so that, mysteriously, the soft misty grey made her eyes glow. 'I should tell you, *your mother* brought along this dress for me.'

He laughed. 'Like hell! Tell me the truth.'

'The truth would not do me much good. Your mother, though a very benign lady, does not like me.'

'Why should she?' He looked down his straight nose at her. 'You scare the hell out of her.'

Morgan frowned. 'I cannot imagine your mother being intimidated by anyone, let alone pint-sized me.'

'How do you know all you know?' he taunted her. 'How can you do all you do? We reckon you have to be two hundred years old. Where do you come from with your great green eyes? How do you transform yourself into a raving beauty in the twinkling of an eye? I swear when I first saw you on the stairs you looked like an orphan.'

'Don't you touch me.' Morgan shivered as his lean brown finger traced the angle of her pointed chin.

'Where?'

Such an answer disturbed her enormously. 'You should not be in my bedroom.'

'Ridiculous,' he said smoothly. 'We're family. Sort of.'

'Bad luck of the draw.'

'Why don't we put our disappointments aside and try to get you presentable? You have good hair. Why have you dragged it back like a coil of rope? I'd only have to give you one little tap to snap your neck.'

'You sound as if you'd love to,' she told him coldly. 'Oh, what's the time?'

'I don't think old E.J. is yearning to be buried,' Ty assured her. 'Step out of that dress, Morgan. You obviously need help with your dressing.'

'Yes, I am a lousy dresser,' she fumed, pulling at her long zipper. 'I can't play at being a clothes-horse. I'm a station hand, remember? I plan to change all that soon. I shall be mistress here.'

'Glorious day!'

'And your last around here.' Morgan tore at her black belt, then stepped out of the offending dress without the slightest hesitation. Ty might not have existed for her, though he leant back against the mahogany bureau watching her every movement.

'All you really need is a gold earring, or maybe a little crown of flowers.'

'You are so wicked, I cannot tell you.' She regarded herself fleetingly in the mirror. There was no question about it, she looked better in the grey dress.

'A little ragamuffin to a dryad whose domain is the forest. Have you ever lain in the grass, Morgan, looking up at a man with those slanting emerald eyes?'

'If you're trying to lead me on about Pat O'Donough, I smacked his face as hard as I could when we were no further than the stables.'

'Is that why I saw you riding like the wind?'

'It's sweet of you, Ty, to be so concerned about me.'

'God knows you'll have every fortune-hunter in the country coming calling.'

'I really won't have any trouble throwing them out.'

'I have to say it, green eyes, you have your wits about you. Now the hair.'

'I'll keep it back,' she told him determinedly.

'I'm sorry, you *won't*!' He reached out effortlessly and removed the long pins one by one. 'Legend has it that Morgan Le Fey had long curving hair the colour of black silk.'

She shook back her head so that a long swathe of her hair slid from his hand. 'I deeply object to your high-handedness, Ty. Let's get out of here.'

'Right away. No need to thank me.'

'You're not exactly my favourite person.'

'I think you irritate me more than anyone else in the world, too. And this is only the beginning. Who's going to look after you now that E.J. has gone?'

They were at the door and Morgan swung around to look up at him. He was tall and devastatingly handsome in his unfamiliar mourning clothes.

'Would you say we were a happy clan?' she asked, almost sadly.

'Come on, we have some good times.' His brilliant blue gaze locked with hers. His hair was a dark gilt with lighter streaks, and his skin had the golden sheen of an idol. He looked what he was: a young man, barely thirty, charged with extraordinary abilities and a passion for life.

'You know I have never felt comfortable with your side of the family.'

'I hope you understand they don't feel comfortable with you,' he silenced her derisively.

'I actually *hate* you.'

'Are you so sure?'

'Yes. I don't *need* anyone to look after me, Ty. E.J. has made me secure for life. I've had an excellent education and I've got a good brain, as my degree testified. You're not the only one in the family who can handle life at the top. I plan to learn, and learn fast.'

He smiled, a humourless movement of his firm yet sensuous mouth. 'I hate to say it, but I've saved your life at least twice. I'm all for a girl's developing her potential, but your drive to prove yourself could have ended in disaster. What the old man did to you was cruel. A lot of grown men would have buckled under the series of challenges he threw out to you. A little girl, five feet two, forced into passing test after test. Is that love?'

'It's all he had to offer.'

Ty groaned. 'My mother, who you think doesn't like you, wept for you. My sisters freely admit they would have been broken like toys.'

'So, I'm the legitimate heir, right?' She tilted her chin with a flash of his arrogant self-sufficiency.

'Don't let's talk about it yet.'

'What?'

'Don't what me, little one,' he returned her curtness. 'I know you're bright, but you're no match for me.'

'Don't make me laugh.'

'You *used* to laugh.' There was affection in his voice. 'When you were so high.' He sketched a level somewhere near his waist. 'You were the most entrancing little girl I have ever seen. Full of magic. All your recklessness never brought you ill luck. Witches aren't frequent visitors to the Outback, but someone sure left you on our doorstep.'

'They must have,' she said sarcastically.

'You bestowed your affection *once*, Morgan. Now you take the most careful handling.'

Derision tilted her mouth. 'I have never noticed your being careful with me. A lot of the time you go out of your way to be particularly hateful. Like today. Anyone would have thought the sight of me offensive.'

'I wouldn't enjoy anyone laughing at you behind their hands.'

'Tell that to your mother.'

He caught her shoulders and actually shook her. 'I expect it was the only damned dress she had. We don't have any elves in our house.'

'And all those females who chase you are as big as amazons,' she said wretchedly. 'It's obvious I need an armed guard around here. Would you take your hands off me, Ty? You're bruising my shoulders.'

'Wild creatures need a little breaking in,' he responded, regarding her with hard disfavour.

'And this is *my* home, if you don't mind. Stick to your own world, Ty. This section of it is *mine*!'

E.J. was buried, not in the old station graveyard, but at the place he had designated, at the foot of a prominent station landmark, a sandstone pillar that reared bizarrely from the vast spinifex plains. The body faced toward the desert and no sooner was the ceremony concluded than the first heavy silver splatters hit the blood-red earth. Everyone ran for the cover of the vehicles, but Morgan continued to stand by the graveside, oblivious of the lurid look of the sky and the thunder and lightning that crashed all around her. She had grown up with violent passing storms, and in any case her feelings were so profoundly complicated that she was long past worrying about getting soaked to the skin.

The minister, a kindly man, tried to speak to her, but she shook her head violently to ward him off. She had too much to think about. It was a terrible, terrible thing to be consigned to the barren earth. Yet in a day or so after this early spring storm the flats would be covered with a myriad of wild flowers. They would reach the vertical face of the pillar and cover this fresh mound.

Her relationship with her grandfather was the strongest bond she had ever forged in her life. She didn't really know whether he had loved her, or whether he was capable of love as most people knew it, yet her entire existence had been given over to pleasing him. He had never rewarded her with even a glimmer of softness or indulgence, but she had not despaired. At her own centre was a strength. God knew how she had acquired it. Her

mother was a recognised social butterfly. The father who
had been fool enough to break his neck in a riding ac-
cident E.J. had classed as a weakling. His fatal flaw was
that he had not inherited E.J.'s peculiar brilliance. E.J.
had been a mighty empire builder; but who could desire
such a thing when he lay buried, not mourned but with
silent sigh of relief? Surely a man would always lack
love when he could not give it. What had caused E.J.'s
inner desolation? His perceived rejection as a child?
Being passed over for a golden young stepbrother? Her
grandfather might not have loved human beings, but he
did have a special affinity with the lonely, timeless
grandeur of the desert.

Morgan's hair ran in slick ribbons. The grey dress was
soaked. Red mud from the grave was running over and
into her soft leather shoes. For an instant she felt terribly faint, as though her loss had drained her of her
habitual fight. She was an actress, of course. She wasn't
really as tough as everyone thought. If only her father
had lived. She struggled with the emotional desert of her
life. As a university friend had once suggested to her,
though she came from one of the richest landed families
in the country, she had much to be depressed about. She
had never been able to enjoy a single laugh with E.J.
unless it had been something bitter and sardonic. There
had been none of the shared joys of family. She realised
now that E.J. had deliberately kept her from her golden
relatives. He had enrolled her from the beginning in a
rival boarding-school and, though she had made friends
quite easily, no one had ever been allowed to visit her
at the Hartland stronghold. She was the heiress with the
traditional dilemma. The poor little rich girl, con-
demned to loneliness and isolation. Not even Marcia
came to visit, though she kept in touch with her in-
frequent replies to Morgan's long letters. Another girl
might have been very seriously affected, but Morgan had

some power from her inner self. Many a time she thanked God for it.

I only need You, she always said in her prayers.

The new world that might have opened with her immediate and instinctive attraction to the young hero-figure Ty, E.J. had gone out of his way to destroy. Was it possible a man so feared and respected as her grand-father could be jealous of an adolescent boy? That was the truly frightening thing about E.J. He had seen Ty as his logical and fitting heir, but this only made his terrible resentments surge up. Did a king really hate and fear his successor? What was she thinking about? *She* was E.J.'s heir, wasn't she? His only grandchild.

Someone came for her before she took root.

'Leave him to heaven, Morgan,' Ty called loudly above the thunder. 'I'll never get over what he did to us. Not in a lifetime!'

A kind of terror E.J. might hear them made her slump against Ty's lean, powerful shoulder. He looked down at her pale, drowning face, the glazed eyes, then lifted her high in his arms.

'You little fool! He wasn't worth all this suffering.'

The Hartland women, not wanting to risk water damage to their impeccable image, were already seated in the big green station-wagon that had brought them to the grave-site. Now they looked out in horror as Ty carried a distraught-looking Morgan to join them. She was waving her slender arms in the air, for all the world like a witch being prevented from casting a spell.

'Get in,' Ty ordered tersely, getting one hand on the doorhandle.

'Not yet!' She almost leapt out of his arms. 'I'm going to walk and walk. What's the matter with you people. We've just buried E.J.'

'And good riddance,' Ty returned balefully.

'I'm not going, Ty,' Morgan cried wrathfully, oblivious of the storm and the pelting rain. 'As God is my witness, I'm going to walk back to the house. I don't even care if a tree falls on me.'

'A hit on the head might be good for you,' he replied savagely. 'All right, if you won't come, I'll walk with you.'

'Ty, *darling*,' his mother called in distress, 'if Morgan must walk, let her. She'll come to no harm.'

'You think so?' He pushed an exasperated hand through his rain-soaked hair. 'If she fell in a pot-hole she could drown.'

'Ty, for God's sake,' his sister, Sandra, protested, 'you know Morgan swims like a fish.'

Ty ignored her. 'You drive, Sandy,' he said. 'Let's face it, I can't let her do it alone.'

'Oh, do please get in, Morgan,' Cecilia begged. 'You're calling such attention to us.'

'I'll get soaked, Ty,' Sandra wailed from the back seat.

'The blasted things that concern you,' Ty lashed out at her. 'Buy another pair of shoes.'

'Please do as Ty says,' Cecilia advised her daughter quietly. 'I knew from first thing this morning that it was going to be a terrible day.'

While the beautiful, immaculately groomed Sandra battled with the elements to make it to the driving-seat, Morgan swung away. She had no intention of following the long procession of vehicles; she would walk uphill, holding on to the acacias, and take the path to the creek-crossing. The creek would probably be running deep by this time, but in one place a series of huge boulders formed a natural bridge. There wasn't an inch of Jahandra she didn't know.

She had scarcely gone a dozen paces before Ty caught up with her, his elegant black suit liberally spattered with red ochre.

'I beg you, don't be stupid enough to try the creek,' he gritted.

'Don't worry about me, Ty,' she called. 'I can take care of myself.'

'Let me tell you, I'm prepared to knock you out,' he cried forcefully. 'The creek will be running a bumper.'

'There's the crossing.' Even fighting with him was an invigoration.

'I fear for you,' he exclaimed wrathfully, and caught hold of her arm. 'Don't you know you've used up your nine lives?'

They were standing facing each other in all the drama of the storm, both of them soaked, both apparently oblivious of it, as their blood filled with anger and pain and the underlying queer excitement.

'I've got many more in hand,' she told him. 'Why didn't you go with your mother and sisters? They are so dependent on you as the big strong male, it must be a real pain.'

'I wish to God you had a little of their helpless femininity,' he charged her. 'I can promise you you won't see thirty if you don't get yourself in hand. The way E.J. brought you up shows how hostile he was to women. You were reared as a boy. A little bitty kid was abandoned to an old crazy. You ask me to mourn for E.J.? Well, I'll tell you I despised the old tyrant. And you know the *main* thing I despised him for? What he did to *you*. Do you realise your whole life has been a kind of terror?'

'You bastard!' It was so shockingly, painfully true, Morgan saw it as brutality. She brought up her two hands and began to beat at him with her clenched fists.

'Stop that!' He got hold of her under the elbows, lifting her off her feet. 'Another word and I'll throw you over my shoulder. How does that grab you?'

'It comes with the name.' Her green eyes glowed brilliantly in a drowned face. 'There's no way a Hartland could be anything *else* but a bastard!'

'If you really want to get back to the homestead in safety, do you think you could be co-operative enough to leave this all to me?' Ty muttered harshly.

'Please yourself.'

'That's impossible, Morgan. Believe me.'

Though his touch disturbed her, she did not resist him when he took a firm hold of her hand. Had things been different between them, even on this terrible day, it would have been a wild sort of delight to be pulled up the hill in the driving rain. It was a silver-grey world of swirling mist as the cold rain hit the hot earth and the birds chittered madly from their shelters in the winging trees. The wind was driving the foliage sideways and, though it buffeted Ty, his tall, powerfully masculine body sheltered her from the worst of it.

When they came down on the creek, the scene to Morgan was beautiful beyond description. Here, under the intense shelter of the trees, the driving wind was a dull roar but its force was abated. The trees, the water-lilies, the verdant green of the reed-beds, were washed clean, and a sparkling silver wall of water gushed from upstream and rushed into the lower levels, crashing against the mossy boulders, creating miniature water-falls. Ducks, apparently too exhilarated to take off, were dipping madly up and down like small boats in a storm, their plumage enamelled by the windswept waters. It was as though the creek, dormant through the dry, was receiving a great boost of power. Overhead, but well away, a great fork of lightning tore the heavens asunder, so that even the air vibrated with the tremendous thunderclap.

'For God's sake!' Ty grabbed Morgan and held her to him as a great white light sprang up through the coolibahs to be followed by a peculiar yellowish glow and the smell of sulphur.

'That's E.J. passing,' Morgan whispered against the hard wall of Ty's chest.

'I don't envy whoever has to put up with him,' Ty yelled, just as though he had heard her, when now the wind rushed deafeningly through the great stretch of passage.

It was the huge coolibah they had often sheltered beneath when day storms were flying about the stations. Surely an omen? Had E.J. passed to the Sky World or the Devil's Place? Morgan pulled away and rushed down the gentle slope to the creek. There was something hypnotic about water. Something marvellous, enticing. Perhaps when she came back in spirit form she would elect to take the form of an undine melting away into emerald pools.

She cast off her ruined shoes, moving now with speed and agility. Life was as turbulent as the flash-flood waters sweeping the long line of billabongs that made up the creek. She was soaked to the skin. What did her dress matter? What did anything matter, come to that? Jahandra was hers. She would rule it with justice and mercy.

Just as the wall of water hit her slight, supple body, spinning her sideways, Ty grabbed her from behind, pinning her like a child as he sorted out the best way to proceed. Like Morgan, he was finding a kind of exhilaration in the savagery of the storm, and the expensive clothes he wore meant nothing to him. The flood level was rising very fast, and he knew very well that without him she would have been swept off her feet and carried downstream. Not that it would have bothered her. Morgan had lived all her life with danger.

In a way it was a kind of insanity. Debris in the form of fallen branches was now being carried along by the increasingly churning waters. When he had them safely out, Morgan, for all her recklessness, found herself palpitating against his arm like a spent bird. His body was warm and vibrant with power. Such physical strength a man had. Such a vast reservoir of untapped energy! The fact that she was revelling in his strength was a mystery to her. As a child she had adored him, his quick wit and his charming manner, the way he was so tall and fearless and handsome. When she first came to read of the exploits of Alexander the Great, she always visualised him as her golden cousin, Ty, Robert Tyson Hartland, the one E.J. had really wanted for his heir.

'It's a good thing I'm so prepared for your madcap behaviour,' he said explosively, releasing her so that she fell back against a tree.

Morgan only laughed, straightening up and reaching for the long wet silk of her hair and pulling it away from her face. 'Another thing you can hold against me.'

'Of course, it's part of your attraction,' he said tightly. 'Let me look at that. You've scraped your arm. It's bleeding.'

'Oh, don't worry about it, Ty.'

'Damn you. *Show* me.' It was obvious he felt like shaking her.

Slowly, without a word, she held up her arm and he turned it to look at the soft blue-veined inner skin. A thin gash about three inches long was oozing tiny beads of blood, and as she stared at him in shock he brought down his mouth and drew gently on the wound.

'No!' Her face flushed with colour and she felt an unbelievable panic.

'Antiseptic.' He looked up, catching the extent of her inner turmoil.

'It could make me *die*!' She was talking utter nonsense. Still she stared back at him in horror.

'What are you *really* frightened of, Morgan?' he asked her somberly. 'Some powerful magic?'

'Frightened?' Her emerald eyes flashed.

'You're giving every indication you are.'

'I didn't realise you were a vampire.'

'Then you're a fool.' His eyes were very blue and very searing. 'Maybe I hunger for a little affection.'

'No, Ty.' She shook her glistening hair. 'I have no tender feelings for you.'

He gave an ironic smile. 'So why are you panting when I touch you? Why have your eyes grown so strange and enormous?'

Morgan drew in her breath sharply. She felt a surge of some primitive emotion, something alien. She backed a little and came up against the pale bole of a ghostgum. Her grey dress was clinging to her like a gossamer second skin, moulding a body so fluid and sensitive that one could perceive clearly its naked form. Her olive skin shone golden, her raven hair, rain sequined, hung wild and loose, and her slanting, luminous eyes held an expression of bright fear, out of keeping with her character.

She was trembling now, while he stood quite still, watching her.

'It's all right.' He held out a hand to her as though there was nothing unusual about treating her like a creature of the wilds.

She stepped forward, though her senses were tremendously alert. The deluge had eased to light rain and the predictable shining arch of a rainbow fell through a blue rent in the heavens to the earth below.

'Come here to me.' His voice was very quiet and gentle.

'It has stopped raining. Almost.'

He cupped her triangular face between his two hands, and while she stared up at him in a kind of thrall he lowered his head and kissed her. Not on the temple, or cheek, as sometimes among company he did carelessly, but on the tiny black beauty spot an inch from her mouth.

She closed her eyes. She didn't respond, but she could not break out of the trance. He kissed her again. This time along the delicate line of her jaw. It was all so terribly *strange*, but she couldn't move. She, the fearless, had been rendered without power. His mouth feathered along her high cheekbone, brushed her pencil-fine, slanting brow. She turned her head slightly and his lips touched the other side of her face. Lightly. She was not completely sure what was happening. What was behind this impossibly sweet, dangerous ritual? Ty was opening himself up to her. Why? After years of hurt, all they had done and said to each other, was his affection disguised?

Only it wasn't affection. Not on his part. Nor hers. This yearning without end was physical. *Passion. Desire.* What was happening to her was not a demonstration of affection, but an exquisitely sensitive seduction.

Seduction. As the word tore through her brain, Ty suddenly put one arm around her, half lifting her off the ground as his slowly questing mouth abruptly covered her own. She gave a trembling gasp and tried to shut her teeth, but this thing that was between them would not allow her. Not yet. She felt a tremendous rush of dark pleasure. Something very powerful and voluptuous. His tongue reached out and caught hers in a love play where no love was allowed. By degrees she was going under. Possessed by a forbidden rapture. He couldn't, shouldn't be kissing her like this. She shouldn't allow it. Only her body, revealed beneath its thin covering, was visibly responding to such unprecedented stimulus. Her slight young breasts lifted and seemed to swell, nipples peaking like thirsty buds.

She wanted ... She wanted ... God, she *wanted* ...

'Ty!' She wrenched her mouth away, her fine skin grazed by the faint rasp of his.

It seemed to be as difficult for him. She could see the shock in his densely blue eyes.

'Wasn't this inevitable?' he asked finally, his tone brittle enough to crack. 'That was straight out of a fantasy.'

'It was crazy. We've gone a lifetime fighting.'

'That's not true!' he said, so fiercely that it startled her. 'When you were a little girl I could pull you on to my knee any time I wanted. Only the old man made sure we were parted. By the time you were thirteen, you yourself started to sow the seeds of rejection. You wanted no other emotion but hostility. In-fighting. Something like that. You'd discovered there was terrible pain in caring. What amazes us all is how easily Marcia gave you up. The old man must have had some powerful hold over her.'

'A good thing I'm such a very independent person,' Morgan said offhandedly, her mind dominated by far more pressing emotions. She felt enormously depressed, yet over-stimulated. Her habitual antagonism towards Ty was no more than a warning system. Some biological defence in the presence of his threat to her. The fact that he had now kissed her, and like *that*, put their relationship on an even more stressful plane.

'If you're willing to walk back to the house like that?' His blue eyes swept her from head to toe.

'Look at yourself.'

He shrugged, as arrogant and handsome as a fallen angel. 'Funerals aren't really my kind of do.'

'What about will readings?' she asked.

His eyes were like jewels in a black-velvet setting. 'Let's face that when it happens. You're gong to need help, Morgan. Bright as you are, you're going to need all the support the family can give you.'

'Forget the family,' she said sharply. 'You mean *you*. Your mother and sisters vote just the way you tell them.'

'I'm unlikely to tell them to do anything unfavourable to Hartland interests.'

'Hartland interests mean you at the top. I know how important you are, Ty, to all our operations. You've built on everything your father left you. You even showed E.J. there was more to wheeling and dealing than even he knew about, but you just might discover the highest you're going to go in the Hartland Empire is being my deputy!'

Ty looked down at her, her drenched appearance emphasising her physical fragility, and a small smile played around his lips. 'God save the Queen,' he mocked her gently. 'Don't let's worry about possible usurpers now.'

CHAPTER TWO

THE house was crowded with people when Morgan came downstairs again. Her hair hung long and gleaming around her face, and this time she wore violet. She had so few clothes. E.J. would have been bitterly offended to see just how many were laughing and coughing very quietly into drinks. It was like the start of a cocktail party. Keep your balance, Morgan thought. A few sincere ones have just got to be here.

There was a traffic jam at the front door and Morgan could see Pat O'Donough's red head as he fought to get to her.

'Morgan!' He was by her side, separating the mourners, revellers—whatever—by virtue of his bulk. 'Why, Morgan,' he clasped her small hand between his, 'you're so pale. You look as if you're going to faint.'

'Not yet, I'm not.' From her vantage point on the stairs, Morgan could see Cecilia's smooth blonde head as she ushered the more important visitors into the drawing-room. Rich and beautiful Cecilia, as sensual as a Rubens. That was where Ty got his extraordinary sexual aura from. The twins, handsome as they were, didn't have it.

'Come down here to me,' Patrick fussed. 'You know how I feel. My heart grieves for you.'

'I appreciate that, Pat. I really do.'

'Oh, sure,' he sighed. 'I know you don't really think you need anyone, but you do. You need a friend.'

'As a friend, you're a wash-out, Paddy,' Morgan told him.

27

'You may be right! God, I'm in love with you. Doesn't that mean something?'

'Thanks, Pat,' Morgan removed her hand. 'Have you got a drink?'

'Mum and Dad are here,' he told her. 'Naturally they want to pay their respects.'

'I had no idea E.J. had so many close friends.'

'I honestly don't think he had a friend in the world,' Patrick mused without malice. 'Apart from you, sugar.' His tawny gaze sharpened. 'How come you and Ty just mooched off?'

'Some people like to be alone after they've buried their loved ones.'

Pat took her elbow and led her down the remaining stairs. 'Yeah, sure. Except Ty loathed E.J. They were really building up to something, weren't they, those two?'

'Some men spend their entire lives jockeying for control,' Morgan replied, nodding gravely to the many people who looked her way. All of them had made the natural assumption she would be named as Edward Hartland's heiress, which automatically made her one of the richest women in the country.

'I wouldn't trust Ty if I were you,' Pat bent his curly red head to whisper near her ear. 'Or the family. They're all set to move out of Tyson's Landing and into Jahandra.'

'You've always been jealous of Ty, haven't you?' Morgan reminded him.

'Why the heck not? He diminishes us all. You know, don't you, sweetie, he's the one old E.J. really preferred?'

Morgan turned on him so suddenly that he fell back, much as he would if a silky terrier suddenly snapped at his heels. 'Ty's a man, a real man, to be sure. And I'm a woman. I can't change that, but let me tell you, Ginger, I am perfectly acceptable as E.J.'s heir.'

Pat gave in immediately, flushed and embarrassed. 'You're a little trimmer,' he said with a glassy grin. 'You'll make some man a wonderful mate.'

'But not you!'

'I could take care of you, my darling.'

'Excuse me, please, Pat,' Morgan said forcefully, 'there must be some way I can get all these people out of the house.'

In the end, it was Ty who actually hastened the mass exodus.

'Everyone understands, I know.' He looked at them, smiling remotely, like a prince.

Of course they did. Where E.J. had been thoroughly disliked, Ty had the charisma of a superstar. His looks alone made an indelible impression, and he had everything else besides: voice, grooming, manner, exceptional ability, the natural, high-mettled self-confidence of a man who had been born a personage. He was the despair of every match-making mother.

Henry De Lisle, E.J.'s only worthwhile friend, partner and solicitor, was staying on at the house and he spoke to Morgan with genuine affection and sympathy. 'What matters most, my dear,' he told her, 'is that your whole life is in front of you. You know, I told your grandfather many times I didn't approve of your upbringing. It would have rattled a lesser person right to the roots of their being, but somehow privation made you strong. E.J. was incapable of showing any outward emotion, but I want you to know he was proud of you.'

'I had the feeling he was always prouder of Ty,' said Morgan ironically.

'Ah well, my dear.' Henry shook his balding, silver head but didn't deny it. 'It took E.J. a very long time to realise a woman could be strong. He always thought looking after houses and having babies was woman's business. To be absolutely specific, E.J. saw women as powerless in the scheme of things. He was of the generation who never contemplated giving women charge of anything outside parties.'

'Then I must have been some kind of experiment.' Morgan fixed her green eyes on him.

'I guess you were,' Henry replied, his voice quiet. 'When would you like me to read the will?'

Morgan shrugged. 'After dinner, please.'

It was almost ten o'clock before they moved into E.J.'s study, a large, depressing room with heavy panelled walls and ceiling, and housing a wide selection of guns and weapons, a strange standing circle of spears and trophies from the hunt.

'God, isn't this an awful room?' Claire drawled. 'I nearly throw up every time I come into it.'

'Dreadful!' her twin echoed disgustedly. 'If I were you, Morgan, I'd heave every stick of furniture out of the house and get the decorators in.'

'I'm not sure I'd do that,' Cecilia said mildly. 'Many, many things are extremely valuable.

'I detest Victoriana myself.'

'I hope that means we're not going to fight about the furniture,' Morgan murmured. 'Aren't you going to sit down, Ty?'

'May I humbly decline?' He bowed at her, six feet two, dynamic male, flaunting his arrogant male beauty.

'It isn't very polite,' she said shortly.

'*Do* sit down, darling,' Cecilia said. 'Beside me.'

Henry, seated behind E.J.'s massive, dust-coated mahogany desk, because no one, not even Morgan, dared go near it, wiped his glasses and put them on his nose. The bridge of his nose had almost disappeared, so they slipped to the tip, but this did not prevent him from opening out the official-looking document, the last will and testament of Edward Jonathan Whitelock Hartland.

'Gee, I hope he left me something,' Sandra said wistfully. 'It would be just like the old devil to have left me that moose's head.'

'We have only just buried him, Sandra.' Henry clicked his tongue.

'Can't you wait for the dust to settle?' Ty asked.

'I guess I won't mind giving you the old moose,' said Morgan.

'Dandy, just dandy.' Sandra gave a wry grin. 'I do wish Ty hadn't told him to shove it so often. You're going to end up with the lot.'

'Oh, I think you're all right, Sandy.' Morgan's luminous eyes glowed very green. 'Furthermore, it wouldn't hurt you to be poor.'

'If we're going to be informal,' Claire defended her twin, '*you* have to think about getting some decent clothes, Morgan. You're starting to look like something from Lifeline.'

'All right, girls,' Ty said mildly. 'That's enough. Henry is wanting to start.'

'Just one thing,' Cecilia begged. 'Please don't start calling poor old Edward the deceased, Henry.'

'All right, Cecilia, I won't. We all knew him.'

Ty rocked back on his chair. 'Yes, indeed,' he said drily.

Henry looked at Morgan for a moment, then began. In a room full of beautiful, golden people, the landed aristocracy, blessed with every possible good fortune, she looked more and more like the denizen of another world. She had always been slight, and the shock of E.J.'s sudden death had rendered her ethereal. Henry didn't know exactly why, but he always expected one day he would turn around and catch her when her wings were clearly visible. Hadn't Ty always called her an elf? There was no denying she had an enchanting wild beauty. What he was going to do to her now made him sick to the stomach. He thought he knew every rotten thing there was to know about E.J., yet a codicil had been added, one he had not known about.

* * *

Don't worry, you're dreaming, Morgan thought. It's a terrible nightmare and you're going to wake up.

'Well, that's the gist of it,' Henry said. 'The twins get parcels of shares, as you do, Cecilia. Much larger, of course. Bequests to the staff. A few to the larger charities. Apart from that, Ty gets sixty per cent of the entire Hartland Holdings, Morgan gets the remaining forty per cent, and they have equal shares in Jahandra homestead. E.J. has further stipulated that both must reside here, otherwise each forfeits their share to the other. Ty, as E.J.'s heir, would need to remain on Jahandra to administer the station, in any case. Jahandra is, so to speak, the jewel in the crown.'

'It's not legal!' Morgan shouted.

'Darling girl!' Cecilia looked across at her with pity.

Morgan leapt up. 'I tell you, it's not legal. I am E.J.'s only grandchild. Is that right, Henry?'

'Surely there aren't any more shocks in store?' Ty asked.

'Shocks?' Morgan swirled, long hair flying in a raven cloud. 'You got to him, didn't you, you devil?'

'You think that?' Ty stared up at her, blue eyes hooded in a fashion Morgan well remembered.

'I will fight this!'

The twins said nothing, fidgeting with their long beautiful fingers, enamel-tipped.

'Please, dear, we sympathise,' Cecilia stood up.

'Maybe it was your idea?' Morgan asked. 'You're one hell of a sexy lady.'

'Agreed,' Ty said tightly, 'but I don't think it worked on E.J.'

'You're upset, Morgan.' Cecilia waved a restraining hand at her adored son.

'You bet I'm upset,' Morgan shouted, tears starting to roll down her pale golden cheeks. 'Jahandra is *mine*. God knows I've paid for it. I'll never, *never* share it with Ty.'

She ran from the room, heart pounding, desperate. She was going to go into a violent seizure. How could E.J. have done this to her? He was unhinged, unstable. She had plenty of money now for lawyers. She would fight them. Ty, with the hunger for power in his eyes; Cecilia, in her elegant black suit, marvellous pearls at her throat, a diamond brooch on her lapel. Impossible to guess her age, Cecilia. The golden goddess with the calm façade. Schemer for her son. The family dripped with schemers.

She didn't even know where she was going. The house was no longer hers. It was Ty's. He had absolute power over Jahandra, Tyson's Landing, Muruk Muruk, Emerald Downs in the Territory. He wasn't even thirty and he was filthy rich and powerful. More powerful now than even E.J. had been, because he controlled his mother and sisters. He would never, *never* control her.

Morgan rushed into the night, for once blind to the great jewelled vault of the sky above her. The aborigines on the station were staging their own wake. At least they respected the dead. Not that E.J. was finally dead until they staged the mourning ceremony. He was supposed to be watching over his close relatives, while his spirit double waited for him at the Dreaming site.

Watching over his relatives! Morgan could have shrieked. She might have shrieked for all she knew. No one would hear or take notice. The air was vibrating with the women's wailing, praises sung at this time of the great Byamee, the white chieftain who was making his long journey to the diamond-encrusted sky.

Oh, what a terrible man you were, E.J. Morgan's heart was beating in time with the spirit drums. She had never in her life felt such acute emotional stress. Not even when Marcia had left her. Marcia was no one's idea of a conventional parent. Neither was E.J. of a grandparent. It couldn't have been more shockingly apparent. To a very

large extent she was the victim Ty had called her. Except
for her courage.

Control your emotions or they will control you.

How often had E.J. said that to her? Even in old age
his striking looks and his power were clearly evident.
Except E.J. *had* no emotions. Someone had cut out his
heart long ago.

As ever in times of stress, she found herself heading
towards the stables. Horses were the only really nice
people she knew. The only ones she loved and admired.
Now that E.J. was dead, she would take Sultan. She
wanted a strong, impetuous ride. There wasn't a thing
she didn't know about horsemanship, and Sultan was
the boldest, noblest horse on the station. Lots of people
said horses couldn't talk, but Morgan had ridden horses
that could talk a blue streak.

Why wouldn't they talk to a leprechaun, anyway?

Ty had said so many things. Robert Tyson Hartland,
master of Jahandra. The very thought of it was driving
her insane!

She was just heading under the archway that led to
the stables complex when Ty came after her with giant
strides. He grasped her shoulder abruptly and brought
her to a shuddering halt.

'If you think I'm going to stand aside and let you
break your neck, you're a lot crazier than I thought,'
he said furiously.

'Would you get your filthy hand off my shoulder?'
she shouted. 'I was here first. These are *my* horses. They
love *me*. Immediately you leave I'm going to tell them
all to kill you the minute you jump on their backs.'

'What could be fairer than that?' he retorted. 'Let
them throw *me*, Morgan, if there's a single horse that
can do it. I feel differently about you. You cannot go
for a three-mile gallop at night. The consequences could
be disastrous.'

'Now isn't that weird?' she cried scornfully, with plenty of fire. 'For once you haven't thought this out. Surely a night ride might put the brat out of the way for all time.'

He literally loomed over her. 'You make it sound attractive, but people can read between the lines. I can't afford to have your violent demise on my head. It would generate too much publicity. Come back to the house, Morgan. *Please*. Mother and the girls are terribly upset.'

'Like hell they are!' Morgan hit out at him in anger and frustration, hurting her hands. 'This has to be one of the most profitable nights of their lives. As if you Hartlands haven't got enough, E.J. had to leave you more!'

'We *are* family.' He caught her flailing hands and held them firmly.

'Ooh! Family, indeed! Family who keep a very strange profile. You never had one civilised conversation with E.J. in your entire life. Though he pretended he was furious with you, he must have admired your guts. A lanky kid standing up to a man famous for his harshness. He always said your sisters didn't know anything beyond spending money. It seems to me I've had to go without all my life while you Hartlands have lived in the lap of luxury.'

'Are you saying we haven't had our own tragedies?' he asked her in a voice as angry as her own.

'Don't go looking for sympathy from me. I was right there in the front line when they started handing out tragedies. I lost my father. You lost yours. Our kind of life is really quite dangerous. My father had been riding all his life, yet a fall from a horse killed him. How many times did your father fly to the capital and back? You couldn't even begin to count, but one trip he just came down in the mountains. I always wondered if he might have been frantic about something. E.J. always drove him. He was such a cruel man.'

'Morgan,' Ty said very quietly, 'I feel the same way.'

'Yet he made you his heir. He deliberately moved to thrust his only grandchild aside.'

'Ah, Morgan,' Ty sighed. 'How do I comfort you?'

'*You,* comfort *me*?' Her great eyes flashed. 'I've known since I was a child that I had to fear you. I knew you'd come after me. It's a powerful tradition in this family, destroying women. You said yourself that E.J. got rid of my mother. He swept her out of our lives. Why? Did he *hate* women?'

'A number of men do,' he told her sombrely. 'You know that, Morgan. I'm beyond trying to fathom what drove E.J. Even you don't know all the facts about him. When he fought, he fought in the most ruthless way imaginable. He showed kindness or affection to no one. There was no woman in his life to soften the harshness.'

'There *was* a woman,' Morgan shouted. 'There was *me*!' Her gleaming hair flew about her small, triangular face. 'He ruled my life with an iron hand. He made it clear I had to measure up in every way, and I did it. You know why? Because *I* was his heir. *I* had to command respect in my own right. I can do anything you can do, can't I?'

His taut expression relaxed. 'Listen,' he said wryly, 'there's no way you're going to head the Cattleman's Union. There's no way you're going to have the same control over all the Hartland employees. These are men who live hard lives out in the open. They're tough. They accept you as E.J.'s granddaughter. They accept you as a true Hartland and they'll show you all the respect they do all our women, but let's be realistic, Morgan. When a man looks at you, he sees first a beautiful girl. A moment in your company and he would next see the substance. Your intelligence, your spirit and character shine through, but you will never, ever, no matter what you do, acquire the status of a man. Your woman's body is against you. I know it hurts. Men will do anything for a woman, except work for her.'

Even in the midst of her anger and confusion Morgan could see the bitter truth. But it did not dispel her rage. 'Nice try,' she said with admiration, 'but let me tell you, when I give an order around here, it's obeyed.'

'Sure.' He inclined his gilded head. 'But the men on Jahandra love you for what you are. Most of them have watched you grow up. The older ones made you their little pet. They had a wonderful time watching you master every trick in the trade. They feared for you when E.J. pushed you over the line. They really hated what he did to you, but they were obliged to keep quiet. E.J. was a dictator. He relished power and he used it in ways no one could condone. He even managed to get rid of your mother.'

Morgan hid her grief under hard flippancy. 'Well, she didn't love me. Most people will accept money.'

'Your father's will left Marcia secure,' Ty pointed out harshly. 'It couldn't have been money.'

'Well, what was it?' She flung up her pointed chin. 'How did he pay her off?'

'Didn't you ever ask her?'

'I couldn't!' It was out before she could think. How did a child go about asking why she wasn't loved? 'There's nothing to Marcia. What you see is what you get. It costs Philip a mint just keeping her in face creams. Looking great is her full-time job. That's all he wants from her, anyway. She's just another carnation to wear in his lapel. No wonder I hate men.'

'You don't. What you desperately need is the right man in your life. Someone who can bring you love and understanding and joy, above all. Your short life, from beginning to end, has been struggle.'

'Yes, hasn't it?' she cried acidly. 'Grandfather taught me to take the reins. Now, when I'm ready, he has subjected me to even worse restrictions. Do you really think I'm going to kowtow to you?'

'Why should I, when the only thing that gives you pleasure or enjoyment is asserting your independence? You're mistress of your own fate now, Morgan. You can do anything you wish.'

'Does this mean you're hoping I'll move out?' she flared.

'That's a fine question for someone who considers us wildly incompatible.'

'I'm going to fight this, Ty,' she warned him.

'Don't waste your time.'

'I can find some top-level lawyer,' she challenged.

'Frankly, they don't come much better than Henry.'

'Henry betrayed me.'

Ty remained immobile, staring down at her. 'Henry told me himself he was knocked for a loop. He has always thought of himself as your godfather. God knows how many times he intervened with E.J. because he couldn't tolerate his treatment of you. And me. He dreaded doing it. He's such a reserved, fastidious man, but he's human. E.J. wasn't.'

'I'll say this for you, Ty, you're a natural-born winner.' Morgan shook her head.

He looked at her quizzically. 'Do you really think life has been so easy?'

She could feel the tears on her face. 'So it was unfair to lose your father. So you've always been burdened with an extraordinary amount of responsibility. So what? You thrive on it. You thrive under every kind of condition, good or bad. Did you know E.J. was going to take care of you?'

'In what way?'

'To hell with you! *Leaving you in control?*'

'You think it was the wrong decision?' he taunted her. 'E.J. was a tyrant, but he wasn't a fool.'

'Oh, I *hate* you!' she gasped.

'Let me go on. He couldn't risk leaving the empire he built up to a woman. Not even a woman. An inexperienced girl.' He pulled her to him and leaned back wearily against the archway. 'Don't fight me. Not just now. I didn't know he was going to do it, yet on another level I knew he would. You simply don't have the strength or the vigour to run a string of stations.'

'What the bloody hell would you know?' Morgan dashed the tears from her cheeks.

'Do you really think you can compete with me for the top job?'

'You bet your life I can. I'm working on it.'

'But I've already perfected it. You can't catch up, elf.'

'I could have hired people. Top people.'

'There can only be one person to give the overall direction. I know how smart you are.'

'Don't patronise me, Ty Hartland.'

He shook his head. 'I'm not. Is power what you really want? Is running a pastoral empire getting the most out of life?'

'*You* want it.'

'Hell, Morgan!' He shook her. 'I'm a *man*. I'll never accept being a captain of industry is a woman's role. Think for a moment. Didn't you really want to be boss so that you'd be one up on me?'

She threw back her head. 'You're absolutely right! Don't try and make out a reasonable case, you rotten son of a gun. You've been aiming for this all along. You're a man of ambition. There's no way you'd walk two steps behind a woman. E.J. would have understood that. He wouldn't have considered it either. Did you taunt him with it some time? No one in this world made E.J. so angry or made him think. He would have mulled it all over. No matter I'm his only grandchild, no matter he saw you as a rival, a woman just wouldn't do.'

'That's right, Morgan,' he agreed quietly. 'A woman won't do. All the people we do business with would get mighty anxious if you showed up as boss.'

'I'm going to take you up on that.' She gritted her small teeth.

'You're not the boss.'

'If I were you, I wouldn't talk too soon,' she warned him. 'What an unscrupulous devil you are, Ty.'

'I guess I am, yes. There's no way I was going to stand around letting you make the wrong decisions. Even if you were a man, Morgan, you have too much to learn.'

'So you set about pointing that out to E.J.'

He laughed without humour. 'Don't let this embitter you. You've got more than enough going for you as a woman. You can lead a rich life. Not so much rich in the material sense. I mean you can lead life to the full. You can become rich in experience. You'll want to marry, have children. You love the land and everything it represents. You're happy here as few women are. Why in the name of God would you want to drive yourself mad running a pastoral empire? Don't you know it's appallingly hard work?'

'That's why you planned on moving into the job.'

'Not really,' he replied coolly. 'What I planned was moving you out.'

Morgan was up with the dawn wind; it was a strange, soft sighing that wafted through the homestead windows. She dressed hurriedly in her daily uniform: cotton shirt, moleskins and riding-boots. Her cream Akubra with the fancy snakeskin band she left downstairs in the little hallway that ran off the kitchen. The houseboy, Jimmy, greeted her with a bowed head and downcast eyes, a thoughtful gesture designed to acknowledge the pain in her face.

'You will have tea?' He spoke in a low, concerned voice.

'Not this morning, Jimmy. I'll have something when I come back. Is anyone else up?'

'Mr Ty, of course. I have already served him breakfast.'

'Damn!' Morgan frowned intently. 'Where was he going after that?'

'Maybe to say thank you to the Old Men. Mr Ty appreciates and understands our culture.'

'Yes, he does,' Morgan smouldered. 'I'll tell you, Jimmy, because your people will soon know, Mr Ty has been named Byamee's heir. We must accept it. Mr Ty is now master.'

'But how did you not guess?' Jimmy asked mystified. 'Did not something tell you here,' he lightly tapped his chest, 'that when the master passed, Mr Ty would take his place? He is respected by all.'

'*I* am E.J.'s grandchild, Jimmy.'

Jimmy shook his snow-white head gently. '*Real* power only resides in men. Women do possess unusual wisdom, but the matters of a great station are best left to a man. Men would little trust a woman with that great responsibility. You should fill your life with pleasure now. It was always considered bad Byamee Hartland made you work so hard. You belong Mr Ty now. He will look after you.'

Morgan smiled wryly. An outstanding aspect of aboriginal culture was the superiority of the male. 'It seems he has started already. Pass on to Mrs Larkin that Miss Sandra and Miss Claire only drink coffee for breakfast, not tea. No one need wait for me. I don't know when I'll be back.'

'Very good.' Jimmy gently bowed, his skin a dark chocolate against the immaculate white of his shirt and light jacket.

Morgan crammed her wide-brimmed Akubra on to her head and walked out into the morning. The sun already had a strong drawing power, all the brilliantly coloured flowers in the garden dancing in a blue mirage sea. One of the boys saddled up Sultan for her and gave her a leg up.

'Plenty o'fire, miss!'

'I know.'

'Couldn't count the number o'times he's kicked me.'

'He's a born entertainer. Have you seen Mr Ty so far?'

Archy giggled, rolling his black eyes. 'Ticked me off already. "Archy," he said, "you only got this mornin' to clean up around here." '

'Don't you just love him?' Morgan murmured ironically.

'He's a personality all right, miss. Remember how he used to tick you off?'

'My dear cousin!'

'Happen to know he saved your skin once or twice.'

'Which horse did he take?' Morgan ignored that.

'It was Lucifer,' Archy called after her with a wide grin.

'He would!' Morgan thought darkly. Lucifer was E.J.'s horse. While he had lived.

The budgerigars were out in their thousands, wheeling in bright emerald waves with flashes of gold. A good gallop would ease her unsettled frame of mind. She could not continue to show her hurt and anger. She had expected too much of her grandfather. She had expected her due. Aunt Cecilia and the girls could not be expected to stay more than a day, and she quite expected Ty to return with them. Ty might be E.J.'s successor, but he couldn't be expected to carry out E.J.'s wishes immediately. She had to tread lightly for the time being, until she could find out if E.J.'s will could be overturned. Surely her right to the controlling interest would be upheld by law? She wouldn't really know until she had consulted a solicitor. Obviously Henry wouldn't do. Henry was on the Hartlands' side. How truly odd she never thought of herself as a Hartland. Probably a psychiatrist might explain that it was because she had never felt wanted. How did one construct an identity when the essential ingredients were missing? Her father she barely remembered. Her mother had opted out of her life. Her grandfather had never concerned himself with offering security beyond the material. In sum, she thought of herself as Morgan against the world.

Everything was coming to life in the wake of the storm. The blood-red earth threw up new, aromatic smells as Sultan's hoofs churned up vegetation and flattened the Mitchell grass. Giant butterflies clustered like blue and black flowers across fallen mossy logs, and already the wild flowers were opening up a million radiant little faces. There was no sight on earth like wild flowers on the sand-gravel flats, miles and miles of dazzling gold and white embroidered in great waves of pink and yellow, blue and purple. The colours of the south-west were strong and vibrant, the eternal peacock blue of the sky spread over the desert ochres molten red and orange, the rose and larkspur of the eroded hills.

Somehow she found herself crossing a shallow channel of the creek and riding upwards to the vertical sandstone butte that marked E.J.'s grave. The natives called the natural monument Jinarli, the Old One, and like the other great desert monuments it had the amazing ability to change colour. This morning it glowed like mother-of-pearl, yet at other times of the day the colour warmed to amber, then cinnabar and finally rose-red at sunset.

Morgan slid off Sultan's back and tethered him to the smooth bole of a sapling that bent in respectful homage towards the gleaming sandstone pillar.

For an instant Morgan expected E.J. to speak to her, to explain what he had done, but the only sound was the soft moan of the wind.

Morgan stood for a moment gazing at the grave. *'In the end you, too, deserted me,'* she said in a voice charged with pent-up emotion. This morning spears of all sizes criss-crossed the mound, protection for E.J. until he had reached the other side. Wheeling in a semicircle high above her head was a lone eagle, a deity to the aborigines. It seemed to be performing some mysterious ceremony of its own, a magnificent pagan thing, silhouetted against the deep turquoise heavens.

The rise of an eagle, Morgan thought. Would she ever come to terms with Ty's effortless domination? E.J. had reared her to be competitive and aggressive, then ruthlessly subjugated her to Ty. That was her true place in the scheme of things. Deeply interwoven in her psyche was the terror Ty would take charge of her life. Ty in his full vibrance. At the end E.J. had only been a shadow to his male heir. How did a woman ever come to terms with playing second best? Well, she would have a shot at turning the tables on them all.

For the first time prayer didn't occur to her. She was consumed by her woman's impotence. Why should most of the world fear and mistrust a woman's authority? She would have thought Margaret Thatcher had finished all that. The Outback was a man's world. It was widely accepted a woman could not command the same respect as a man, when splendid women abounded. It was shocking and inherently wrong. She *could* run Jahandra. She *could* make important decisions.

So deep in thought was Morgan, she failed to notice the arrival of a station hand, a black-haired man dressed in a blue denim shirt and levis.

'Miss Hartland?'

Morgan wheeled just as Sultan gave a loud warning whinny. 'Oh, it's you, Adams.' She knew him, of course, but as a rule the men didn't approach her.

'Just came up to pay my respects, Miss,' Adams said smoothly. He was a big, solid man in his early thirties, fairly new to the station, and attractive in a dark, rather coarse way.

Morgan nodded. 'I've heard it said you disliked your boss.'

'My respects to *you*, ma'am,' he grinned, showing excellent white teeth. 'I wouldn't have given the time of day to your old grandfather. He was one hell of a mean man.'

Morgan's face lost its look of strain and flushed angrily. 'Who knows, you might find his granddaughter even meaner. Do you really think you can stand there and criticise my grandfather?'

His face coloured. 'Take it easy, Miss Morgan. I can't see why you would want to defend him. The news is all over the station. Your cousin has been given custody of the Hartland empire.'

'Surely as a man you would approve of that?' she asked steadily.

Adams looped a thumb through his silver-studded belt. 'What makes you think we wouldn't obey *your* orders?'

'I haven't found you particularly polite,' Morgan said, disturbed by something in his expression. He was moving closer, his sheer bulk crowding her. 'I think you should go. You must have work to do.'

His lips twisted in a wry smile. 'You want to smack my face, don't you?'

Morgan was amazed. 'Adams,' she snapped, 'it would not occur to me to touch you.'

'Unless you became aware I could make a great ally.'

'Ally? In what way?'

Adams smiled, his closely set dark eyes running over her with obvious relish. 'I figure you'll need someone on your side. Someone you can trust. A sort of informer. The men talk all the time.'

'And I know just what they are talking about this morning.'

'And how do you feel, Miss Morgan?' Adams asked sympathetically. 'Passed over for a big shot. I understood the two of them were at each other's throats.'

He could see her flinch. 'Have you anything else to report?' Morgan asked coldly.

'Don't get the feeling I'm laughin' at you.' He suddenly checked himself. 'I'm on your side. You're one spunky young lady. Beautiful, too. I think you're capable of running the station. Hasn't Hartland got enough to manage? Just how much does he want of the world? Him and his swanky women. I was happy to just stand there and goggle yesterday. You Hartlands have got everything. Not a one of us don't admire those blonde twins and *you*! If it came to a contest, I'd pick you every time. You're the one to turn a guy on.'

'And you think I appreciate being told that?' She kept her face cold.

'Why not?' Adams asked almost dreamily. 'You're a woman, aren't you? You're so bright and aggressive, you don't understand it's a challenge. I love that little beauty spot beside your mouth. It's almost heart-shaped, like your face.'

What could he be thinking about? 'I think you should get back to your job immediately,' Morgan said with real anger.

'You look beautiful,' he said, and put out a ponderous hand.

'Touch me, Adams,' she gritted, 'and you'll have no chance of survival.'

'Don't you like men, honey?' he crooned. 'The old guys have been so proud of you since you were a little kid. They tell tales about you all the time. They even tell the way your cousin had to rescue you when you were showing off. You've broken a lot of hearts, do you know? Course, all of them would be too shy to approach you. "She's a Hartland. A very high-class lady." But times are changin'. There's you, for example. Thought you were gonna be boss, and all the time old E.J. was laughin' behind your back. Hartland, too. Maybe all that conflict was just kiddin'. Ever thought

of that? You give me your banner and I'll carry it. I
always think of you as a gorgeous little princess.'

Morgan was stunned. 'Adams,' she said sharply, 'I'll
give you one more chance. Go away, and never speak
to me again.'

He rubbed his hands together with sheer delight.
'You're full of passion, aren't ya? Great sparkling green
eyes and flying hair. How the hell could a little bitty
thing like you rule in a man's world? You need protection. You won't get it from golden boy. You oughta
know now, honey, he's the *enemy*!'

'Your enemy, too, Adams.' Morgan stood her ground,
more outraged than she thought possible.

'This is between you and me.' He stared down at her
steadily, transfixed by her expression and that meltingly
lovely mouth.

'That's enough!' Morgan cried furiously. 'You get
your things together. I'll have you kicked off the station.'

His black eyes flickered. 'Is that the little boss talking?
Five feet nothing. Simmer down, honey,' he soothed her
boldly. 'I wouldn't hurt you for the world. You ever been
with a guy?'

Morgan didn't even hesitate. She brought up the whip
she carried and lashed him across the face.

'Why, you little devil!' His black eyes narrowed so
that they almost disappeared. He ignored the red weal
that ran from his left cheek along his jaw, faint tremors
in his solid body. 'Anythin' would be worth it to kiss
you. Touchin' those high little breasts. Know what, you'd
love it. There's so much passion in you, I can tell.'

Morgan eyed him with contempt. 'Just try me,' she
warned. 'If I could, I'd have you shot out of hand. As
it is, you leave. If you think my grandfather was tough,
you had better not tangle with Ty.'

Adams grinned fiercely. 'Want you himself, does he?'

Morgan gasped. 'How dare you?'

Adams sneered. 'Big, handsome, dashing guy. He could have *any* woman, but I think he fancies you.'

'Nothing like that!' Morgan said in disgust. 'But he's capable of killing anyone who would harm me.'

Adams stared at her in bewilderment. 'Who the hell wants to hurt you? One kiss, that's all I want. I'm just fascinated by everything you are. All the time I've bin here, six months, I've never gone a night without thinkin' of you.'

'That's sick!'

'No, it's *fun*!' He reached out and caught her by her shoulder. 'You're a very smart girl, but you've been exploited by men. Your grandfather. Now Hartland. I want to help you. I'm the best man on the station. Didn't old Morrison tell you that? I know my job and I've got a brain. I don't like to boast, but I'm a real success with women. You want to toss that little whip away, honey. You don't need it. We'd make a good pair.'

'Godzilla!' Morgan drew a deep, furious breath. 'Take your hands off me.'

'That I promise.' He bent his head to her. 'Did you know I saw you swimmin' naked one day? Yes, don't gasp. I did. Wasn't where I shoulda bin, of course. Let me kiss you.' His dark eyes blazed. 'Let me peel that little shirt from your back.'

Morgan was so outraged, she forgot to be frightened. Could any man be fool enough to assault her on her own land? She pulled back violently, kicking out grievously, but though he grunted in pain he caught a handful of her long, gleaming hair, jerking her head back.

'I don't want to hurt you. Settle down. I really care what happens to you. Trust me. You're so small, so soft.'

She had gone through her life being taught how to defend herself, but now, though she was making gallant efforts, it was proving futile. He caught her to him with an excited burst of laughter, crushing her breasts.

'I swear I won't hurt ya,' he promised. 'You gotta learn what it's like bein' with a man.'

'You're not a man, you're an ape. A lousy ape!' Morgan felt red rage suffuse her. She groaned aloud as his big hands began to caress her, trying to squirrel away energies for the final ding-dong assault.

With her head bowed, slight and deceptively doll like, she didn't even see the man moving with blurring speed up the slope, but she certainly heard his violent shout.

'Get away from her, Adams.'

The ferocity, the deadly anger of the tone, had the same effect on Adams as a stray bullet. He dropped the hands that formed a bow across Morgan's body and jumped back in startled reaction.

Ty was almost on their level, but suddenly Adams launched his last-ditch offensive. He ran forward with a shout, his right arm lifted high. He was a powerful man, but Ty was advancing with the purpose and speed of a missile. Anger was stark on his face. A primaeval outrage. His blue eyes burned and his tall, lean body took on a palpable aura. Energy bounded off him, an unmistakable menace.

Adams went down like a demolished brick wall and Morgan felt her heart give an involuntary flutter of fright.

'You didn't have to kill him, did you?' She rushed forward to check on the inert Adams, a perverse terror welling up in her in case Ty should be the one in trouble.

'Leave him!' Ty jerked her away.

'He's all right?'

'I said, leave him,' Ty repeated so angrily his teeth snapped. 'What was he doing here?'

'What do you think?' Morgan retaliated, furious at his tone. 'Paying his respects to E.J.'

Ty's voice dripped acid. 'Didn't you know he had an outsize crush on you?'

'How the hell? The yahoo has only been here six months. He's been fairly normal up until now.'

'So what did you say to push him over the edge?'

'I said I loved him,' Morgan shouted. 'I said stick with me and I'll make you foreman.'

Ty's eyes were glittering like glass. 'No one knows better than you how to send out messages.'

'Are you nuts? Tell me. I honestly don't know.'

Ty took a breath, barely keeping himself under control. 'The only way a man could act like that is if you gave him the come-on.'

Morgan thought smoke would come out of her ears. 'How sweet, how glorious! I encouraged Godzilla?'

'When are you going to learn, Morgan?' Ty persisted. 'Women like you ought to be locked up.'

'How absolutely disgusting! Women will never be free of sexual harassment because you *men* are such brutes, beasts, lustful devils!'

'No jokes,' he said harshly. 'Women like you can tear a man to pieces. Tatters. I can make it so that Adams won't find employment in three states.'

Adams, on the ground, began to moan and Ty prodded him into full consciousness with the toe of his riding-boot. 'On your feet, Adams.'

'What happened?' Adams groaned. 'I don't seem to remember.'

'Half-wits have poor memories,' Ty pointed out.

'Son of a gun!' Adams cried admiringly. 'You're the first guy to ever floor me.'

'Want me to do it again?'

'What for?' Adams rose groggily. 'I meant no harm. Miss Morgan and me were just havin' a discussion.'

'More like a brawl,' Morgan said disgustedly.

'I wouldn't advise you to say any more,' Ty warned him tensely, the muscles of his jaw knotted. 'You're finished here. You know that.'

'Isn't that a bit callous?' Adams complained. 'I've worked hard.'

'This has nothing to do with your work. As it happens, you know your job, but no man in his right mind would dare offer insult to our women.'

Adams was shaking his head madly, trying to clear it. 'That's just what I told you,' he protested earnestly. 'I worship Miss Morgan.'

'So does every male on the station,' Ty snapped. 'None of them would ever dream of laying a finger on her.'

'So what do you want me to do?' Adams begged, looking to Morgan for support. 'I'll apologise. It'll never happen again.'

'You bet it won't!' Ty looked so dangerous, Morgan wanted to get Adams away from him. She gripped his arm, feeling the pent-up rage.

'No harm was done, Ty. He was acting kind of nobly. For him.'

'I'm very sorry, Miss Morgan,' Adams offered shrewdly, still affected by that splintering karate chop.

'Get your gear together,' Morgan said smartly. 'I want you off the station as soon as it can be arranged.'

'Aren't you comin' on too strong?' Adams complained, staring at her sadly.

'Get!' Ty roared, exploding so violently that Adams took one look at him and began to run down the slope, gravel skidding from beneath his riding-boots. 'This is between you and me,' he gritted, giving Morgan a scaring look. 'He's the best damn hand we've ever had.'

'Maybe I ought to marry him!' Morgan responded. 'Call him back.'

Ty made a visible effort to control his ferocity. 'Don't let his apology fool you. He's a crude customer. How long do you think it would have taken before he raped you?'

'Raped me?' Morgan cried, almost leaping off the ground. 'I don't expect you to give me any credit, but I could have handled Adams had I chosen to.'

Fury lit Ty's face. 'As it was,' he said violently, 'he was handling you.' His blue eyes fell to her shirt. In her struggle with Adams a button had pulled loose, exposing the golden upper slopes of her breasts. 'Don't you ever wear a bra?'

'Who the hell wears those old things?'

'She who seeks to retain her virtue. I've been meaning to speak to you for a long time. That skinny-dipping has got to stop.'

'Holy hell!' Morgan cried. 'What skinny-dipping?'

'Like in the creek. You're going to deny it? Half the men on the station are terrified they might come on you.'

'That's obscene!' Morgan faltered. 'I want to die.'

Ty gripped her arm. 'You're not a little kid any more. You put a man in a ferment, then you wonder why he goes bananas.'

'High time you started defending Adams!' Morgan tossed her head. 'Men are all brutes.'

He laughed shortly. 'That brute is going to pay for his sins.'

'*I* sacked him,' Morgan flared. 'Don't ever try to stop me sacking anyone.'

'How far did he get?' Ty asked in a low voice.

She wanted to hit him but dared not. 'A lustful bearhug. What are you so angry about? You looked as if you were about to kill him.'

'You'd better believe it,' he rasped.

'Don't make me laugh.' Despite the heat, Morgan's teeth were chattering. 'You'll protect me against all-comers. Who's going to protect me from *you*?'

He glared at her. 'Oh, yes,' he said bitterly. 'I'm a threat without a doubt. Big bad Ty! Why don't you try talking about it to a psychiatrist? I'm the predator and you're my prey.'

Morgan's heart was beating fast. 'Don't tell me there's not *some* sort of struggle going on. Why did you kiss me yesterday? You deliberately tried to arouse me.'

'I didn't have to try very hard.' He studied her without favour.

'You do have a destructive sex appeal.'

'Well, it worked for the day. We don't even like each other, yet something about you awakens the primitive. Maybe it's all those bright challenges you throw out. What do they relate to? Do you want to be dominated by a man?'

'Don't try to psychoanalyse me. It can't be done. I am *extremely* independent. E.J. reared me that way, may his soul go wailing down the ages. This is the kind of conflict he set up. He had to be slightly touched.'

'Come back to the house, Morgan,' Ty said.

'What, my *half*-house?'

'A house that has forty rooms.'

'You exaggerate. It has thirty-eight.'

'Pick any nineteen you like except the study.'

'That's the symbol of power, is it?'

'I'll be damned if I'll try shifting the furniture.'

'You're not going to live with me, Ty. I won't budge an inch.'

'Must you fight the will?'

'Buy me out.'

'And how would you survive away from the place you love? You're giving E.J. a hard time, but he left you very rich. I can't see you in the city, Morgan. You're as wild as the birds. No one could put you in a cage. You wouldn't live.'

'I'll never live with you,' she repeated.

'So, I'll get married. We'll have a proper chaperon.'

'Yes, get married,' she challenged, quivering with a mad rage. 'It would be what the papers call the biggest event of the decade. Phillipa Lynch is quite intelligent and jolly. I don't think I could tolerate Camilla Ogilvie.

You could pick from a hundred girls. I'll be bridesmaid with Sandy and Claire.'

'That's sweet of you, Morgan.' His voice was full of mockery. 'But the idea of you as bridesmaid troubles me. I can see you with a little coronet of flowers and a mad glow in your eyes. Try to deny it, but you'd reject any wife!'

'You go to hell,' Morgan said hotly.

Ty only laughed grimly.

CHAPTER THREE

WHEN Morgan returned to the house, the twins were curled up on the front veranda enjoying morning coffee and the beauty all around them. It was very peaceful on the veranda, looking out over the lushness of the long-established gardens made possible by sinking bores. A summer-house in the Indian style dominated the fore-ground, its latticed sides surrounded by masses and masses of beautifully scented white lilies. Lawns sloped away and magnificent trees overhung broad gravel paths. Birds made such a song as could never have been heard in the city, and the *wompa-wompa* of the drums was still being signalled through the hills. It was magical. Mystical. Part of her.

'Hi!' Sandra, the spokeswoman called. 'You've got so much life in you, you make Claire and me feel like wax dummies.'

Morgan's face softened, they looked so lovely. 'Some dummies!' she said wryly.

'You're not happy, are you?' Sandra asked in a low voice.

Morgan leant back against the white wrought-iron balustrade. 'Did you expect me to be?'

'At least E.J. made you rich. That's a start.'

'Try to understand, Sandy,' Morgan said fervently. 'I am the *only* grandchild. I should not have been passed over.'

'Oh, why do you love the land so much?' Claire wanted to know. 'It's a dreadful thing to see you racing around the station like a jackeroo. And look at your clothes! Do you know you've got a button missing from your shirt?'

'I'll sew it on tonight.'

'Why don't we just split?' Sandra suggested. 'The three of us. We could have a marvellous time in Sydney, Melbourne, head up to the Gold Coast. It's glorious! Hundreds of people. Plenty of life. We know all the right crowd. They're always begging us to bring you, Morgan.'

'What's so great about having a ball?' Morgan asked quietly. 'True friends are hard to find.'

'You need *some* life, Morgan,' Sandra insisted. 'You're getting too reclusive out here. Look at your hands, and don't try tucking them away. You aren't a man. You shouldn't want a man's job. I figure I could turn you into a ravishing creature. Let's head off to the big smoke, and do some shopping. You've never had a decent thing on your back for as long as I can remember. When E.J. zonked out so suddenly, Mamma went crazy trying to find you something to wear. Not that we've got anything your size! Why don't you open up to us, Morgan? We really care about you.'

Morgan nodded. 'E.J. kept us deliberately apart.'

'Why do you suppose he did that?' Claire asked. 'I mean, it was a bit much, wasn't it? After all, cousins usually stick together. We wanted you to come to our school, but E.J. made sure you went somewhere else. We used to brood about it for hours. Whatever happened to him to make him so sour on the entire female sex?'

'Not having met his mother, I wouldn't know.'

'Hon,' Sandra said promptly, 'I suppose this sounds like I'm completely on my brother's side, but I'm not. I'm a female. I have a heart. But do you *really* want to take over? I don't understand it myself. You think it's easy making all the tough decisions? The right decisions? Can't you imagine all the endless frustrations of a girl trying to do a man's job? Not just any man, a man born to take control. Though they never did anything else but fight, Ty would seem to be the obvious choice. He'll keep it all together. It's of vital importance he should. We know you're a whole lot brainier than us. Claire and I aren't set on big careers. We genuinely love our life as it is. Our family is wealthy. We have an established social position. One day not too far off, we'll marry. Probably we'll choose husbands we've known for years. What is it *you* want to do?'

Morgan had no hesitation. 'I want to serve in the capacity for which I was trained. I was reared to believe I was my grandfather's heir. It's not overwhelming ambition. It's my *right*. Can't you see that?'

Claire groaned. 'Don't for God's sake go into that feminist stuff. It's depressing, I know, coming off second best, but don't you believe in your heart that Ty is the natural heir? Speaking as objectively as I know how, I would have to say Ty has a far higher status than you. He's brilliant, he's impressive, bursting with ideas. Damn it, Morgan, he's just the sort of man you'd expect to rule the earth. I'm not saying it because he's my brother and I love him dearly. Ask anyone in the entire Outback. Ty's the man. He's as prominent on the scene as ever E.J. was. It's tradition, don't you see? The man is the boss and I for one don't want to fight it. There's more to life than working your butt off. There's travel, romance, dancing, parties, family. You'd look marvellous in the right clothes. You're so highly individual. You could create such an image. *We* could create such an image. You couldn't be more unlike us physically. Instead of twins, we'll make up a trio! What do you say?'

'I say I intend to try to reverse E.J.'s will,' Morgan told her firmly.

'Listen, Morgan,' Sandra said kindly. 'Give yourself a break. Don't fight Ty. So you two strike sparks off each other! It doesn't mean that he doesn't care about you. God damn it, he loves you. I know it's difficult to believe, but he cares about you, Morgan. A lot. Your fortune, our fortune is all tied together. Ty is a whizz at business administration. Why do you really suppose E.J. left him in control? Not to spite you, though he was a pretty spiteful character—in this case it was his deep feeling for his own empire. All that he had built up. Giving you the upper had would tend to restrict Ty. Ty makes restrictions fade away. In a contest, you would be bound to get hurt.'

'Except I am not being given the opportunity to be put to the test. I agree Ty has earned a great deal of prestige and respect, but bypassing me is not justified. I *can* do the job and I feel I can do it well.'

'Oh, come off it, Morgan.' Claire sighed deeply. 'You're not the dynamo Ty is. We know you've run the place as E.J. got older, but lately Ty has been making all the big decisions.'

'How is that?' Morgan challenged, eyes brilliant.

'Ask Ty. He has all the evidence. Men are strange creatures. Every one of them. When it really comes down to it, they'll trust a man before they ever trust a woman. Even women trust men more. Face it, Morgan, it's a man's world. A few women have their moments, but it's not easy on them. Some opt for careers over marriage and motherhood, but then they get to mid-life and realise something terribly important is missing. My advice to you is to accept this. It would have been ghastly if E.J. had not taken care of you, but he did.'

'What, splitting the house down the middle?' Morgan laughed without humour.

'And that's another thing. None of us wants to be separated from Ty. He's the sun we all circle round. How are we going to stay on at Tyson's Landing with him here? We're a close, loving family. Mamma would be lost without Ty. She depends on him so much.'

'So why don't I go to Tyson's Landing?' Morgan suggested derisively.

'Can't we live together?' Clare asked tentatively.

'My ego demands I'm the boss,' Morgan pointed out laconically. 'How stupid of me not to realise you would all miss Ty.'

'I couldn't stand it!' Clare wailed.

'How glorious to be so blinded by love!'

'Oh, come off it, Morgan,' Sandra said. 'It would be too much to have to go back to Tyson's Landing on our own.'

'Take your brother with my blessing.'

Conversation came to a halt as Cecilia walked out on to the veranda. 'Aren't you going to have breakfast, dear?' she asked Morgan. 'It's really not a good idea to miss it. There's nothing of you.'

'What there is is tough!' Morgan went forward so that Cecilia could kiss her. 'I don't feel terribly hungry.'

'Nevertheless I've asked Cook to serve breakfast out here. It's so very beautiful looking out over the garden. It's a credit to you, Morgan.'

'I think we should do the place up,' Sandra said. 'This could be a real showplace. You're so clever, Mamma.'

Cecilia turned. 'Aren't you forgetting, darling, this is Morgan's home?'

'Don't forget Ty,' Morgan said, looking at Cecilia directly.

'Can't we all sit down?' Cecilia gestured Morgan into a chair. Her voice was as soft as usual, but full of a long-established command and authority. 'E.J.'s will created a few problems, to say the least. I understand very well how you feel, Morgan.'

'Forgive me, Cecilia. I don't think you do.'

Cecilia shook her magnificent golden head. 'One day I'll tell you how my family came to lose Tyson's Landing. A few years later my father died. Of heartbreak. You're very young, Morgan. I want you to know you're not the only one who has known suffering and confusion. I know you're a clever girl. I know your abilities haven't even begun to be tapped, but the fact of the matter is you couldn't begin to command the same amount of respect as my son. In rearing you as a boy, E.J. has almost alienated you from your own sex. You were reared to have grand, not to say impossible, expectations. Not the reality of good prospects. Some field a young woman of ability could excel at. You were bred to believe you could take over large-scale responsibilities, in many ways a hazardous life. Men die in our way of life, as you know. Had it been truly necessary, perhaps you could have made a go of it. For a time. But, Morgan, the stress would have worn you out. Men do have a tremendous high-energy output. Look at Ty. Look at you with those dark shadows under your eyes. There are very real differences between the sexes, dear. Not only biological. I think it's high time you took your proper place. You have a great deal to offer, I know. If only you and Ty could work together. We all acknowledge your brain and your intuitive good sense, but as you must know running a pastoral empire is just one of those jobs best left to a man. It would take you a very long time to grow into the image of power. And do you really want that? Can't your contribution be on the human side? There is so much you can do as a Hartland. You know I have many projects dear to my heart. We have a responsibility to help others. I could certainly do with your help. You don't have complete control, Morgan, but you will have tremendous say in all Hartland operations.'

'Oh, yes,' Morgan said drily, 'I'll have my say. But who will listen?'

'Ty is a far cry from E.J.,' Cecilia pointed out. 'Ah, here's Cook, with your breakfast. Henry would like to have a word with you before he goes back.'

When Morgan looked into the study she found Henry seated behind E.J.'s massive desk, going intently through some papers.

'You wanted to see me, Henry?' she asked, taken by the whole tragi-comic situation.

'Please, Morgan, come and sit down.' Henry stood up and came around to the leather chesterfield. 'There are some small things for us to talk about, business, but mainly I wanted you to know that I had no idea your grandfather had added that codicil to his will.'

'I'm going to fight it, Henry,' Morgan said promptly.

Henry brought his long fingertips together. 'My dear, you won't win, but you could split the family.'

'How do you know I won't win?' Morgan's green eyes rested on Henry suspiciously.

'It would never come to court. E.J. knew what he was doing. Most people would agree Ty is the logical choice. That includes most Outback families, you know. There would have been outrage had E.J. not provided for you in an appropriate manner, but acceptance will be evident as soon as the word gets around. Ty is enormously respected, as you know. Which is not to say you are not an exceptionally able young lady. No one could fail to recognise your intelligence and your obvious beauty, but you can't overlook Ty's force. He's not yet thirty but he's a man to be reckoned with. You have no such reputation and it would take you a very long time to build one up. Consider trying to reach tough cattlemen, buyers, dealers, competitors. You would have to work tremendously hard just for them to recognise the brain behind the face. Can't you see some of them roaring with laughter when they're confronted by a young woman of your seeming fragility? They won't see the grit underneath. They won't even look.'

'Resistance. Resistance. I know, Henry. It all sounds very reasonable and convincing, but Ty could just as well back *me*!'

'Ty has got into the habit of command. One might say it's inbred.'

'It seems that way. You think E.J. made a wise decision, don't you?'

Henry patted her hand. 'At first I was affected by what I saw as E.J.'s treachery, but I've slept on it, Morgan. I'm very fond of you both. You and Ty. If you would only stop feuding you could mesh beautifully. It would be interesting to see that happen. You could divide up responsibilities. Act more effectively in allowing each other natural ground. It could make for a much easier and pleasanter life. You work too hard. So does Ty. Men die earlier because of stress. You could be a tremendous help to Ty, as he wants to be to you, yet you do everything in your power to try him. E.J. threw up barriers. He couldn't easily countenance the affection you had for Ty. To put it in a nutshell, he was jealous. He always saw Ty as his rival. He wanted to isolate you and he did. Except things changed when he knew he was dying. He had to leave his empire to the one he judged the stronger.'

'What comfort! Ty and I have been rowing for years, now he has chained us together.'

'Maybe he recognised you would make a great team.'

'Does a team go to war?' Morgan asked. 'Why was E.J. such a hard, hard man? You knew him better than all of us, Henry. Why was he so desperately unlovable?'

Henry considered. 'Because love passed him by. He was treated cruelly, you know, as a child. His stepmother was a beautiful woman, but from all accounts she had a mean soul. Robert was the apple of everyone's eye. E.J. was brilliant, but Robert had all the charm. Afterwards E.J. never mastered handling affection. He couldn't communicate his emotional needs, either. In the end, the stony mask became the face. That was his tragedy.'

'But we *all* suffered,' Morgan said bleakly. 'Look at what he did to my mother.'

'Ah, yes, your mother,' Henry said carefully. 'You haven't seen much of her, have you?'

'To be completely honest, Henry, she doesn't particularly care to see me. Not every woman oozes mother love.'

'It's a mystery to me. I'm sure we're overlooking something vital. Marcia was completely intimidated by E.J. He was very stern and domineering with her. Your father showed a lot of courage marrying her when E.J. ran everyone's life. Cecilia, of course, was a Tyson. One of our oldest landed families. E.J. had an Ogilvie picked out for your father. It was all about business, you see. Furthering his empire. And it goes on. Louise Ogilvie is trying desperately to arrange a marriage between Ty and her eldest—what's her name?'

'Camilla. I wouldn't want to share my house with Camilla Ogilvie, though she's just the sort to join the family.'

'I doubt that she would want to share her house with *you*.' Henry coughed drily. 'The ideal arrangement would be for you and Ty to get married.'

'Out of the question.' Morgan reacted violently. 'Could you really see Ty and me together?'

'Now that you ask, I could,' Henry answered mildly. 'It seems to me, if you would allow yourself, you could pick up where you left off. I recall a time not all that long ago when you hero-worshipped Ty.'

'He was a lot nicer then,' Morgan pointed out bluntly.

'Ty hasn't changed,' Henry said. 'Now, if you could come around to the desk, I have a few papers I would like you to sign. Now that your grandfather has gone I'll go into complete retirement. If you take my advice—and, Morgan, I am devoted to you—you will allow your affairs to remain in our hands. My son Richard is the senior partner. He has been handling the bulk of Hartland affairs for some time. Richard is extremely able. He is also very loyal and trustworthy. A lawyer in the finest tradition. So many young people these days go into law for the money. I can't agree with it at all.'

*   *   *

Ty himself flew Henry to the point where he picked up a commercial jet to fly back to Sydney. Bernie Adams was shipped out, silent but unrepentant, on the regular charter flight bringing in freight to the station.

'So what did he do?' Sandra asked, agog. 'I thought he was shaping up well.'

'So did he,' Morgan shrugged. 'I don't suppose you and Claire want to chase up brumbies in the morning?'

'Brumbies!' Sandra threw up her hands dramatically. 'The things that excite you, Morgan. How did you come by that reckless streak?'

'The job has to be done. I can remember the time when you two used to love a gallop.'

'Not after brumbies; they're too cunning.'

'We have to go after the lead stallion. It's lured two of the station mares away already. There's a big herd roaming, smashing down fences, drinking the precious water, eating more than a domestic animal. Some of them we might be able to domesticate, but the rest! They're worse than donkeys.'

'And they're dangerous, Morgan. Have you spoken to Ty?'

'I'll be damned if I'll speak to Ty,' Morgan told her shortly. 'Hudson and the boys know I'm coming.'

'You're still going to have to check with Ty. Remember, my girl, he's on the job already.'

'And I was on the job long before him.'

'Morgan,' Sandra sighed, 'you're awful!'

Cecilia did not interfere in any household arrangements, so dinner was served according to long-standing ritual. E.J. had been a sparing eater all his life, but he had insisted on being served prime Hartland beef every night in various guises. Fish and fowl were not for him, but rare beef and plenty of home-grown vegetables, nary a pudding or dessert. No delicious calorie-laden gateaux, no sumptuous ice-creams with sauces. Fresh fruit was tolerated, and a cheese platter to finish off the always superb dry red wines.'

'God, this is dreary,' Sandra moaned. 'Doesn't Mrs Larkin know anything about *haute cuisine*?'

'On the contrary, Mrs Larkin *does*, but E.J. wouldn't allow it. He never took much notice of the theory one shouldn't eat too much red meat, yet perversely sugar was out.'

'It wouldn't have hurt him to have had a sweet tooth,' Claire observed. 'Haven't you ever noticed the relationship between people and their diets? Is there anyone who won't touch sugar who isn't sour in some way?'

'Well, that's not your problem,' said her twin.

'Cecilia,' Morgan said quietly, 'you're not eating. I'm sure Mrs Larkin could make you up something else in moments.'

'That's all right, dear, I'm not particularly hungry. I was wondering what was keeping Ty.'

'There are always last-minute instructions. Probably he has countermanded mine.'

Ty joined them less than five minutes later, apologising for his late arrival. 'What's this I hear about going after some stallion?' He threw Morgan a sharp look.

She nodded composedly. 'A big grey. He's been after the mares. Cheeky devil. He comes in very close.'

'You weren't thinking of joining in, were you?'

'Try to stop me,' she said. Without even thinking, Ty had taken E.J.'s place at the head of the table, filling the ornately carved oak carver with distinction and style. He looked stunningly, vibrantly handsome, looking up to smile at his mother as she placed his meal before him from the selection of covered dishes on the warming trolley.

'Good ole Hartland beef!' he murmured laconically. 'I really prefer a side salad when it's hot.'

'I shall instruct chef,' Morgan said sardonically. 'I guess there are going to be lots of changes around here.'

'You bet!' His blue eyes dazzled her. 'You know going after brumbies is quite dangerous? Depending on how strong and how wild they are, they can break out of any trap. Tom Brennan was killed when a mare kicked the fence down and went right over the top of him.'

'I'm only in on the chase,' said Morgan crisply. 'Mustard?'

'For God's sake, haven't we got any strawberries and cream?' Claire asked. 'Peaches would do. I like something sweet.'

'Peaches it is.' Morgan jumped up and went to the buzzer that connected with the kitchen. 'Tinned, I'm afraid. Plenty of fresh cream. I can't remember the last time I had strawberries.'

'Gosh, you've led a dull life! It must have been ghastly, just you and E.J. You poor little thing! I never realised just how grim it really was.'

'At least the wine cellar is superb.' Sandra opened her blue eyes wide and smiled. 'Do you suppose we could have a Sauterne?'

'Who are you asking? Me or your brother?'

'Don't be difficult, Morgan. You do it so well.'

Mrs Larkin, plump and motherly, came into the dining-room, her hands respectfully clasped.

'Claire is afraid to speak, but she wants peaches, Mrs Larkin.'

'Very well, miss.'

'And cream, Mrs Larkin. I do like to finish with something sweet,' Claire added coaxingly.

'Why not, miss? I always do. Peaches with a little dash of Cointreau.'

'We'll have to start getting up a whole lot of new menus,' Morgan said drily.

'Which brings us to where are we all going to live.' Sandra's lovely face creased into a frown of anxiety. 'Ty is our brother, Morgan. We can't lose him.'

'Really? I'd enjoy that very much.' Morgan threw a look at Ty, handsome as a young god in a mythology book.

'Be serious,' Sandra begged. 'What are we going to do, Mamma?'

'Return to Tyson's Landing, of course,' Cecilia said gently. 'It's a lot more comfortable than this.'

'Gosh, Mamma, it would only take you a couple of ticks to turn this into a palace.'

'I know this is new to you, darling, but Jahandra homestead belongs to Morgan and Ty.'

'Don't you want us to move in?' Sandra begged, blue eyes bright and luminous.

'Someone will have to move in,' Morgan responded tartly. 'I have my reputation to consider.'

'I agree,' Sandra upheld her. 'We don't want any gossip.'

'We've been chin deep in gossip all our lives.'

'Who's asking you, Claire?'

'What do you think, Mamma?' Claire asked, for all the world as though Morgan had no say at all, or she would defer to Cecilia as they did.

'I think it will take divine wisdom,' Morgan intervened. 'Ty, please put your entire family out of their misery.'

He finished his glass of wine and set it down. 'The family could move in temporarily. Until I get married.'

'What?' The twins cried as one as was their habit. 'Then you've been lying to us. The things Camilla has been saying are *true*?'

Ty laughed shortly. 'I have absolutely no idea what Camilla has been saying.'

'She says you're on the verge of asking her to marry you,' said Sandra.

'Well, not quite.' His thick lashes veiled his brilliant blue eyes. 'What do you all think of the lady?'

'I have complete confidence in her to make you the perfect wife,' Morgan said sweetly. 'Under *no* circumstances will I tolerate her at Jahandra.'

'I could have sworn half of it was mine.'

Cecilia took a deep breath. 'This will of E.J.'s has put us all in a difficult position. It will be hard for Ty to administer Jahandra in the way he would want from Tyson's Landing. Jahandra is the outstanding property in the chain. In any case, Morgan's wishes are paramount. It's true you do need someone living here for appearances. There's Aunt Maggie Tyson.'

'Good heavens, Mamma, Aunt Maggie would drive Morgan bonkers.'

'Funny thing, I don't mind her,' Morgan said. 'If she gives me any trouble I'll lock her in the basement.'

'Are you never serious, Morgan?' Claire asked.

'The problem is I'm always serious. Aunt Maggie is a real Outback character, but I've learnt one thing. I have to be my own boss.'

'Of course.' Aunt Cecilia regarded the small triangular face gravely. 'Have you any suggestions of your own?'

'I have no idea about how you feel leaving your home, Cecilia. You're a beautiful, gracious woman. I can't see you playing second fiddle to any woman, let alone me.'

Cecilia waved that away. Even the movement of her long, shapely hand was an event. 'Morgan, I'm convinced you're a very superior young woman. I would forecast that within a year or two you're going to establish quite a reputation for yourself. I know Ty is going to do everything in his power to turn the two of you into an invincible team.'

'Cecilia, what a pitch!'

'My dear, I am quite serious. If you would only give Ty your full co-operation the results might surprise you. E.J. has a lot to answer for. Right at this minute I don't think he's hearing good news. He did everything in his power to alienate you from the family. The really strange thing is he never succeeded. I would have found it a very easy matter to mother you, Morgan. I longed to do it but feared to interfere. Still, I spoke to E.J. several times a year to no avail. Finally I had to stop. Whenever I spoke, the isolation increased. Ultimately he was trying to part you and Ty.'

Morgan's fine forehead creased. 'I know that, yet he has tied us together.'

'He was nutty enough,' Sandra said morosely. 'Why don't we vote on it? I guess it's all up to Morgan, but I wasn't aware we couldn't all get on together. We women, I mean. Mamma will have to separate Morgan and Ty.'

'Fabulous!' Ty said boldly. 'Mamma's first job of the day will be to stop the crazy yelling. I don't want to think of how Morgan's going to get in the middle of station decisions.'

'You think *you're* such an expert? You'll have plenty to learn from me,' Morgan fired.

'Could we call a truce just for a moment?' Cecilia suggested quietly. 'This is a huge house. We could all find our privacy, yet offer each other the traditional support. The arrangement would only be temporary to see how things would work out. Morgan retains the right to say at any time she's not happy with things. Ty will marry and I hope it's not too far off. I suppose I shouldn't say this, but I really hope it's not Camilla. Her family simply can't conceal their greed.'

'Besides, she borrowed my mink jacket and never gave it back,' said Claire.

'May I sleep on this, Cecilia?' asked Morgan. 'I know this probably sounds hard, but I don't feel in need of comfort at the moment. I would like to stand on the top of a mountain and scream my frustrations.'

'I know just the place to take you,' Ty suggested, looking at her so steadily that she had to look at him.

'In case you're interested, I've left a letter to say if anything happens to me, arrest you!'

'Partner!'

'I would like to return to Tyson's Landing for a few days,' Cecilia continued, undeterred. 'That's if you decide we'll stay together for a while. I would like my nephew Steven and his wife to come from Muruk Muruk to oversee the place. Ty?' Cecilia looked at her son.

'I'll go along with that,' he agreed calmly. 'In fact I'm counting on Steven's support. Alan Thomas will move up one. I've already got things started.'

'You didn't call on me for approval of the appointments?' Morgan lifted her delicate slanting brows.

'I didn't consider you'd disapprove.'

'How high-handed can you get?'

'Do you disapprove, Morgan?' asked Cecilia.

'No. I just wanted to be informed.'

'I don't believe this,' Sandra said, giving Morgan and her brother a wide-eyed stare. 'Why does the air crackle around you two?'

'Lots of people have a catastrophic effect on one another,' said Morgan.

Cecilia touched a hand to her elegant chignon. 'E.J. had the care of Morgan for a very long time. We won't find harmony overnight.'

Morgan was still roaming around the house, sleepless, after the family had retired to bed. Her movements were sharp and quick, full of a brittle, nervous energy. She wandered from room to room, a small girl, wrapped in a jade silk kimono exquisitely decorated with blossoms and birds. Her narrow feet were bare, padding softly over marble and parquet and marvellous glowing Persian rugs woven with dense floral patterns, medallions, arabesque birds and animals of the hunt. Most of them were late nineteenth century and of the finest quality. They had never received any care, but they were remarkably sturdy. But the twins were right. The house looked like a mausoleum, while Tyson's Landing was a wonderfully open and sunny place, an inspiration to anyone who wanted to know how to live well. Cecilia had excellent taste and the money to indulge it, but she disliked anything that looked 'done'. So did Morgan. There was such a depressing feeling about Jahandra homestead. She supposed that could be altered very simply by changing the dark colouring of the house. E.J. had been adamant about leaving things the way they were. In consequence, a general air of gloom and faint decay lay over the huge rooms. As a house in stone, it was very stern and formal, in complete contrast to the picturesque timber colonial mansion of the Tysons'. Even the paintings were very Old World, dark interiors that would probably look marvellous properly lit. Baroque-like drapes hung at every window, extravagantly be-tasselled, in rich, deep colours but drawn so close together that the sunlight barely touched either the heavy furniture or the works of art. She had to admit it all came to life at night when the innumerable chandeliers performed miracles. She had a sudden longing to clear everything out and start again. Nearly everything could be used again, but in a different way. One of life's pleasures was deriving comfort from possessions long associated with family. All the dark, sombre, rather severe beauty could be lifted by someone with a strong sense of style. She hadn't the slightest doubt Cecilia could transform the place to something extraordinary, but she wanted to do it herself. There was one huge stumbling block, of course. Ty. Ty, and this mysterious shadowed figure who would be his wife.

Morgan shivered as though a particularly chilly wind had blown through the house. Ty's *wife*. Her legs seemed to turn to marble and she came to a halt, staring at herself in the central mirrored panel of the elaborately carved wall. Her hair streamed over her shoulders and her eyes looked huge, dominating her face. Who had had those slanting eyes? In her experience, such a distinctive feature had to be handed on by a parent. Ty's stunning looks and overwhelmingly blue eyes came from Cecilia, that radiant sexual quality that both had which could never be acquired. The twins owed their looks to both sides of the family. All the Hartlands were fair, including Morgan's own father. Certainly Marcia was a brunette, but her eyes were a soft grey and set straight on. Although she wasn't in the least Oriental-looking, as Ty sometimes teased her, she did have a decidedly exotic look. Russian? She had a picture of a Russian ballerina with slanting eyes like hers. Morgan lifted her fingertips to the corners of her eyes, staring at herself as though she expected the girl in the looking-glass to answer her.

'Who do you expect to see?' a voice asked from behind her.

'A devil!' She spun around to face him. 'I thought you had gone to bed.'

'I was waiting for you to go up.'

'Don't wait for me.' Morgan shook back her long hair. 'I'm used to wandering around half the night.'

'That doesn't surprise me in the least,' he said softly. 'The witching hour is coming up.'

'Who do I look like, Ty?' she asked seriously.

'Whoever it was, they were as exotic as hell.'

Her eyes flew to him. 'What do you mean, whoever it was? It must have been Marcia's side of the family.'

'Raven hair is a rarity in our side of the family. So are green eyes. I mean, they are very, very green, aren't they? As deep as emeralds.'

She sighed and turned back to the mirror. 'Mirror, mirror, on the wall, are you going to buy all that?'

'Don't you ever feel you should have a talk to Marcia?' asked Ty, moving silently across the room to stand directly behind her. 'Here, do you want me to lift you up?'

'I can see.' And so she could, from the shoulders up. Much more of Ty was reflected, the gilt of his skin and hair, his blue and white printed olive-bronze shirt. Whatever he wore became an ornament, just as it did with Cecilia. Looking at them both was an experience.

'Hi, elf!' He reached out and stroked her hair.

'That's going back a bit.'

'You don't look any different.' His expression was amazingly indulgent.

'What should I talk to Marcia about?' She pulled her hair over one shoulder and began to plait it, still facing the mirrored wall.

'I have the feeling Marcia could tell some melodramatic story.'

'Marcia?' Morgan said stiffly. 'Though I am devastated to say it of my own mother, Marcia is just another pretty face. There's not a great deal to her.'

'Unfortunately, no, but a good deal could have happened *around* her.'

'What are you getting at, Ty?' she enquired sharply. 'Next you'll be telling me I'm illegitimate!'

'A great idea if I want to toss you out, but I have this feeling Marcia might have led a private life.'

'What?' She whirled on him.

Incredibly, he appeared serious. 'Somehow, Morgan, you don't fit in.'

'You'll have to do better,' she scoffed. 'I know what's behind this. You're worried I'm going to contest the will.'

'Why should I deny you the chance to be happy?' His voice was laced with derision. 'Just don't forget Henry's the expert and Henry told you you'd be wasting your time.'

'We'll see,' Morgan frowned. 'I've got lots of money now. I could even get married.'

'Anyone in mind?' he asked lazily.

'Anyone who doesn't remind me of you.'

'Isn't that a bit odd?'

'Not as odd as your trying to seduce me.'

'Charming! I thought it was you doing all the emoting. What do you think of this idea of the family moving in?'

'I hope to sleep on it.' Morgan shrugged.

'The alternative is, the two of us will be on our own. Which is the more difficult?'

'There's always Aunt Maggie.'

'Who, incidently, is one of your greatest fans. Maggie was a feminist before anyone ever thought about it.'

'That's probably why she never married. Let me reconsider. I mightn't either.'

'Whatever you do, you'll have to discuss it with me.'

'Really? I wasn't aware of that.'

'You are now. I have a thing about protection. Which brings me to another matter. I don't want you going out in the morning. As I hear it, the stallion is a rogue.'

'Don't plan on stopping me,' Morgan responded smartly. 'I have as much right as you to go wherever I please.'

'True enough,' he said grimly, 'but there's no good reason why you should put yourself in danger.'

'Forget it,' Morgan shrugged. 'We've had some crazy times together. You'll be around to protect me.'

'I don't want you to go, Morgan.' He took her by the shoulders.

'Friction already?' she taunted him. 'I've been doing my own thing for most of my life. If E.J. were still here instead of in Devil Country, he'd be giving me an early-morning call.'

'All I can say is the good Lord has been looking after you. I've had to save you once or twice.'

'Don't remind me. I don't want to dwell on anything in your favour.'

'Why not? Why is your hostility so consuming?'

'Because of your ambitions.' She was staring into his eyes. Neither of them was making a move.

'Why, I ask you, are you bent on self-destruction?'

'I'm bent on opposing you,' she said, meaning it.

'So you won't feel what you want to feel?'

Her eyes flickered and her heart began to hammer. 'Will you, for God's sake, stop that?'

His twisted smile glittered. 'Exactly. We couldn't afford to be alone together.'

She honestly meant to push past him, but his nearness, the powerful magnetism of him, pulled her off course. The very worst thing happened and his arms went around her, clenching her to his warm, lean body. Her robe, loosely belted with a silk tie, fell open, revealing the soft, nearly sheer film of her nightgown, the tender outline of her breasts, and swung away to her narrow waist and the tantalising curve of thigh.

Her heart was thudding so deeply, so painfully, she thought she would suffocate, yet her head was falling back, her mouth upturned. She was tragically, infamously, teetering on the brink of temptation, unable to speak when her body was communicating its need at the most powerful and primitive level.

'Morgan!' His tone was severe, constrained, as though he too was at the mercy of the physical hunger between them. Both seemed frozen, as though they would perish before surrendering to the rage that was in them, and she gave a parched little moan, attempting to soothe her mouth with the tip of her tongue.

One little action, yet it brought him to flashpoint. His control was overthrown. His handsome face, set in taut lines, became that of a conqueror. If passion had mastered him, he had to bring his own authority to bear on her. He folded her to him in a hard triumph, cushioning her raven head against his arm while he successfully captured her mouth and crushed it into subjugation.

Morgan was already defeated. She had always known in her heart this was going to happen to her. That one day she would enter that forbidden doorway. Known and hidden from the knowledge. Ty was the best and worst of her. Wasn't that why she had begun in desperation to build up defences? Hostility was her shield, her armour. The incendiary sparks that flew between them represented her way of warding him off.

The assault on her mouth, brutal and stormy in the first moments, passed into an exhultation of the prize. His mouth ravished her, delighting in her cushiony lips, the play of her pointed tongue, the taste of the sweet, moist interior. Her response was high-strung, reckless as she was. This thing between them was ungovernable, a rampaging fire.

His hand brushed her breast, exciting her beyond bearing. Not content, his hand of its own accord slid under the soft lace of her nightgown, and with its advance her flesh tautened. She wanted to cry stop, but her voice was hushed, every nerve leaping beneath the satin sheath of her skin. Such a thing was unprecedented, yet her body was quivering quite beyond control. The ministration of his fingers brought the tender, highly sensitive nipple to radiant life. She was breathless, gasping at the sensations it induced. Her eyes beneath the closed lids were flickering wildly as sexual excitement welled deep within her and shot flame-like to her limbs. She wasn't even sure if her feet were on the ground. He was supporting her totally, his mouth moving down her throat and back up again to her mouth.

His mouth tasted of her, a faint perfume hung in the air and clung to their skin. Against all her long training she was pressing herself against him, feeling his arousal and the trembling muscle of his powerful, lean body. She wanted her bare flesh against his. Not this thin covering of clothes. She wanted to feel her breasts against the hard wall of his chest. She wanted . . . she wanted . . . She couldn't handle what she wanted. She was excited, in a dazzle. There were bubbles in her blood.

He caught her under the knees and lifted her off the floor, his down-bent gaze arrested by her wild beauty. She was breathing very deeply, her small, perfect breasts lifting, her nightgown an imperfect covering for her young, yearning body.

What he did now could change everything. His fierce struggle was apparent in the rigidity of his body and his tense expression. He began to move, not actually sure where he was going, not yet in control of the fierce current that fused them.

Her eyes, luminous and huge, opened and her head seemed to float up. She was nothing in his arms. *Nothing.* Yet, slight and soft as she was, she threatened his defences.

'Where are we going?' Her voice was hushed, bemused.

It pricked him into full consciousness. 'Nowhere. You're with me.'

Incredibly she sat up in his arms, linking her arms behind his neck. 'Now we know the truth about one another, don't we?'

'What is it?' he asked quietly, deeply into her eyes.

'We exert some kind of spell over each other.'

'I can't deny that, Morgan. Not now.'

'You had better. Put me down.'

'Are you sure you can stand up?' He slid her down against his warm, vibrant body and she half leaned against him, her forehead resting for a moment against his arm.

'Morgan?' He turned her head up so that he could look into her face.

'I'm all right.' Her green eyes reflected all the brilliance and light of emeralds.

'Don't worry too much because we're human. Let's sit down for a moment.'

He led her towards a baroque settee covered in green and gold brocade. 'I feel so terribly confused,' she said, bending forward and hugging herself with her arms.

'Why, elf?'

'Don't elf me,' she warned, simultaneously affected by the tenderness in his voice. 'How do I know you're not playing some game with me?'

'No games. Promise.' He tucked a long, gleaming strand of her hair behind her ear.

'You're capable of it.'

'What about you?' he retaliated. 'You're full of wondrous tricks.'

Morgan sighed. 'If I had my wits about me I could figure it all out. With you beside me I don't get the chance. It hasn't turned out quite the way we hoped, has it? E.J. in his complexity saw to it that neither of us was the outright winner.'

'Just suppose, to make sense of it, he intended us to strike a bargain and marry.'

'When we can't exchange a civil word?'

He held her incredulous eyes. 'Yet I'm quite acceptable as a lover.'

'Hah!' She leapt up. 'My body might cry out to you, but my mind tells me you're a ruthless character.'

'Oh, I am, and there is war between us, but leaving all that aside, why don't the two of us call on Marcia?'

'What a terrible idea!' Her tone revealed her surprise and dismay.

'Maybe.' He looked at his hands. 'But I'm curious about a lot of things. I've always been curious. Especially now.'

She gave an angry laugh. 'You mean now when I hold so much stock? Not to mention half of this mausoleum.'

'Fix it up and it would be rather nice. Why don't you do something womanly for a change? I've said it a million times. You offend me as a jackeroo.'

'Obviously I have to do something to put you off a bit,' she pointed out witheringly.

'I suppose so,' he sighed. 'This really isn't some kind of ploy. You don't need any more to screw you up. What Marcia and E.J. did to you was pretty dreadful. I'd really like to know why.'

Some expression on his face, the utter seriousness of it, alarmed her. 'Why don't you mind your own business?' she suggested spiritedly. 'Set Camilla's heart on fire. Marry her. That's one sure way of getting me out of the house.'

'And why would I want that? You're such a mad, mad creature, everyone else seems ordinary.'

'Let's face it,' she said scathingly, 'Camilla Ogilvie *is* ordinary.'

'Could it be you're jealous?' His azure eyes mocked her.

'If you want to marry Camilla Ogilvie, that's OK. The problem will be where the two of you are going to live. There's no way I'm pulling out, though I can see now you're trying to force me to flee for my own protection.'

'This is a bad time for it. Did Marcia ever speak to you about your father?'

Morgan looked shocked. 'You're really pushing it, aren't you? Marcia used to send me lots of books so that she wouldn't have to speak to me at all.'

'Marcia was rather used to sexual goings-on, so I hear.'

'Say one more word about my mother— ' Morgan warned fierily.

'And you'll what?'

'I'll wake Cecilia and tell her something has to be done about you.'

'I think she knows,' Ty contributed drily.

'Knows what?'

'You've hung your spell on me.'

'Bunkum!'

'What's the rest of it?' he asked her, a mocking twist to his mouth.

'I'm going to bed, Ty,' she cried emotionally.

'But not to sleep. I've decided to slam on the shower.'

'I'll sleep like a log! I'll be up early as well. To meet you all at the Two Mile.'

'And you'll be sent packing when you get there.' His lean face hardened.

'Then I promise you we'll come to blows. I'll put on such a turn, I'll embarrass you in front of the boys.'

'It's just possible they'll back me,' Ty told her. 'Have you thought of that?'

'No one on the station would dare tell me what to do.' Morgan wavered.

'But now they tell *me*. They fear for your life, Morgan. No, don't fling up your head. All of them to a man disapproved of the way E.J. exposed you to real danger. Ernie told me it's on account of you his nails are bitten down to the quick. Ride around the station, fine. We'll all be delighted to see you, but don't come on this brumby chase. Brumbies are *wild* horses. I know you might have been born on the back of a pony, but even you know there are rogues. Bad 'uns. Killers!'

'I'll be damned if I'll stay at home.'

'And I'll be damned if I let you go.'

'Wonderful!' Morgan threw up her arms. 'Then it's war!'

CHAPTER FOUR

Just as she threatened, Morgan was up early to join in the brumby chase. She had lived all her life out of doors, mustering, boundary riding, helping with the fencing, droving, even making the station kill at times. There was nothing she liked better than being astride a horse, riding with vigour or enjoying the vast, colourful station she loved. Did Ty really think her eventful, exciting life was going to come to a close? She was as courageous as any man. More courageous than a lot of them, as she well knew. What was she supposed to do now? Sit at home reading romances, while the men came and went? She lived for adventure. Adventure wasn't playing the landed socialite like Sandra and Claire. Once or twice she had been allowed to join them in Sydney, going on the non-stop partying, functions, showings, the arts, the whole glittering scene. She had enjoyed it in a way. She loved the opera, ballet, theatre, often far more than her cousins. She had a deep sense of beauty, but she loathed all the noisy parties, the alcohol and the press of admiration. Some women exulted in playing games, in harmless and sometimes hurtful flirting, but Morgan was very sincere about everything. She had the feeling she could use her looks to wield a lot of power, but she was desperate to break loose from the sexual role imposed upon women. She had character and a mind. She was efficient and hard-working. She was responsible for herself.

When she went to her bedroom door, it was locked. She rattled the knob in a frenzy, feeling more violent by the second. What a low-down, dirty trick! Just the kind

of thing a supposedly enlightened male would do.
Women could agitate all they liked, men would refuse
to recognise their right to act as men did in this world.
Who, for instance, would have dared to lock Ty in his
room? Grotesque! His boyhood activities were far more
dangerous than hers. *She* had never been stalked by a
crocodile in the Territory. The crocodile would have
taken her. Ty's boyhood adventure only glorified his
maleness.

It was sickening! No one, absolutely no one was going
to dictate to her, tell her the way she was going to live.
Her eyes flashed and her cheeks flushed. Every rotten
thing Ty had done came back to her. She flung away her
memories of how he had saved her from real harm. She
was quivering with a passionate intensity. Ty could have
saved himself the useless gesture. She would climb over
the balcony, inch her way along the ledge and slide down
the vigorous solandra at the corner of the west wing.
The Cup of Gold vine had grown really enormous. It
reached right up to the roof, heavy with glossy green
leaves and huge golden flowers. It was quite capable of
holding her weight.

Only once she thought she would break her neck, when
a loose board wobbled beneath her foot. She gripped
the balustrade for a few moments and took a deep breath.
It was a long way to the ground. There were a lot of
things around the homestead that needed repair. If Ty's
action this morning was evidence of the kind of thing
he might get up to, she had to get this particular escape
route made safe. She might even get toe grips set into
the wall, something like mountaineers used!

Quite sensibly she had worn gloves, and it was a rel-
atively easy matter to climb out on the vine, her small
booted feet finding purchase on the density of knotted
branches. She could easily make it. But her hand, instead of clenching on the leaf-covered rope, made contact
with the unmistakable slithery skin of a snake.

'Yuck!' She swung out in spontaneous shock, gritting her teeth as she began a small, painful slide. Had the vine borne thorns she could have ripped herself to pieces. As it was, all she suffered was a fright and a too rapid descent to the ground.

She came, trim *derrière* down on the gravel, using her hands to protest herself but badly grazing one elbow. Cute! She had Ty to thank for that. She stood up, brushing herself down. Her elbow looked sore. It certainly felt sore. And tender. There weren't too many women of the eighties who were forced into climbing out of their own home. That was another thing, she fumed. It was her house. Half her house. What the hell was he doing, locking her in?

Jimmy was busy sweeping up leaves in the courtyard, but he looked around in astonishment as Morgan dashed through the stone archway.

'Mornin', miss.'

'Good morning, Jimmy,' Morgan spoke rapidly, realising he would have received orders. 'I'm taking Sultan out this morning.'

'Where ya goin', miss?' Jimmy set his broom aside, taking a close look at her. 'Hurt ya arm, did ya?'

'A trifling thing. You heard what I said, Jimmy.'

'Sure, miss, and I'm gunna help you, only Mister Ty leave a message.'

'Do tell me,' Morgan invited.

Jimmy stroked his broad nose. 'I don't know if ya really ready for it.'

'Me, too. Please tell me all the same.'

'Follow him at your sorrow.'

'That's it?'

Jimmy shook his curly head from side to side. 'Miss, I'd *listen*. Best not go after them. I seen that stallion. He was close enough to shoot. Boom! Boom! Only afore I could find somethin' to shoot with he was gone. With a mare. He's huge. Massive. A grey. Kinda magnificent. Mister Ty will curse ya if ya show up.'

Morgan told a fib. 'I'm only riding to the Twin Billabongs.'

'Beaut!' Jimmy saluted smartly. 'I was worried ya were gunna power away after Mister Ty.'

Power away she did. Sultan, sensing a rebellion, was ready to charge in an instant. Jimmy stood quite still, watching them vanish.

'Come back safely!' he yelled, not at all sure Miss Morgan had been telling the truth.

Twenty minutes later, from a vantage point, Morgan saw the small outfit riding across a gully. Only days before water had raced through there in a way no city person would have thought possible. Flash-floods in the Outback were frightening, primitive, blasting walls of water, but amazingly the water settled and the plains were covered with the millions of paper daisies that now blossomed so luminously. It was a stunning sight from the top of the rise. Almost surreal, like a glimpse of paradise. Often as she had seen the mass display of flowers, her heart lifted every time.

She could catch up the men without difficulty. No one knew Jahandra better than she did. Not even Ty. If she rode down Nightmare George—the name had come from an early explorer's experience—she could make up valuable time. In places the gorge was less than two metres wide, fringed with dense almost tropical ferns, but she never had any trouble getting through. Her rebellion was fed by two sources: her desire to get even with Ty, and her fight for her rights as she saw them.

Morgan pressed on. When you knew how to handle Sultan he was as sweet-tempered as a mare. Birds exploded in their legions, winging alongside them, and soon Morgan came on the first water-hole, the verdant surrounds chopped up by many unshod hoofmarks.

'Hallelujah!' Morgan breathed. There was an army of hoofmarks further up. The men were on the trail. They could have even set up a trap by now or decided on driving the brumbies into the already existing strongly built yards. Mostly these yards were fashioned out of stout logs, at the very least two metres high, driven deeply into the ground and held together by wire. The entrance to the trap was about one and a half metres and it was blocked by four strong slip rails that fitted into slots. Fanning out from the gateway were long, V-shaped wings hidden by scrub. Once the brumbies were in, there was little chance of their getting out. The hard part was getting them to go in. Hard and often dangerous.

The wind whistled eerily through the canyon, with the sun bouncing off the inflammable-looking rocks. A chain of shallow pools, surrounded by water-loving plants, ran cleanly through the centre of the carved corridor from entrance to exit, and the sheer sides rose in waves of spectacular colours: pink, rose, ivory, crimson, indigo. Morgan often thought her desert country had something of the character of ancient Egypt, but, where the pyramids had been man-built, the great desert monuments of the Outback had been fashioned by strange gods. Nowhere was more Australian than the Heartland.

'C'mon, Sultan!' she urged as they rode out on to the dense floral carpet of Batchelor's Buttons. Soon she came on a holding yard and it immediately occurred to her, as it would have occurred to Ty and the men, that when the brumbies started running this was the place to drive them. A quick look around assured her that it was Ty's intention. Everything was in excellent working order and a split in the wire had been repaired and reinforced. She would have to take care now. The brumbies were following water and this area was laced with gullies. None knew better than the wild ones which routes to take through the bush. None dared follow them through thick growth.

On a gibber-strewn ridge-top she got her first view of the herd: the massive grey stallion, leading the way, followed by mares, yearlings, and several foals bunched up tightly behind their mothers. There were about fourteen in all, manes and tails streaming, galloping without caution towards the men who were staked out ahead. Morgan had been with Ty more than once when he had lassoed a fleet-footed brumby they had chased for days. Only the best were retained. Most horses were gelded, rarely retained for breeding. The grey looked magnificent, even if he was a rogue.

Moments later the entire outfit rode from cover, frightening the brumbies so that the stallion reared and plunged, his wild cry filling the air. The mares froze momentarily, waiting for direction, and the stallion came down hard on his powerful legs, seemed to brace, then broke immediately into a thundering gallop, the herd trailing behind. All they had to do was follow the leader, and to Morgan's surprise the number one mare was an ex-station hack. It hadn't taken her long to revert to the wild!

With her blood racing, Morgan raced down from the ridge. She was certain she could help. She had done it before. Even E.J. had found a few words of praise for her, even if Ty had always called her a reckless little fool. Why was her personal safety more important than his? She could ride like the wind. Maybe it was her size. She was built like a jockey.

Across the gold and white plain, a frantic Ernie Hudson had spotted her.

'Gawd almighty!' he roared. Morgan's familiar figure was riding pell-mell towards the herd, enough to make any man go pale.

The warning cry galvanised Ty. 'Stay right on them, then veer right.' His face was like thunder. 'I'll cut her off.'

No need to ask who she was. Ernie's face worked.

Lucifer broke out of the group, hammering up an impressive turn of speed. His ebony tail streamed out like a pennant as they flew across the flat. As the herd thundered towards her, Morgan rode hard to swing them away in the direction of the yard. The outfit were close behind, but Ty on Lucifer was riding straight for her. Even at a distance she could see his face set in a granite mould. It was all tied into his theory that she was useless. Some of the mares and foals had faltered, but there was never any doubt about the big stallion. It thundered on, its sides heaving like bellows.

'Clear out!' Ty waved his fist furiously at her. 'Out of there, Morgan.' To do so would be to lose incalculable face. Domestic horses would have run right into the yard, but wild horses, like any wild creature, were a whole lot smarter.

The stallion sensed not only danger but the holding yard ahead. Just as the men were closing, turning them straight for the yard, the stallion suddenly broke, a stark reminder of its spirit and fantastic cunning. The mares and yearlings were being gathered in with whinnies of terror, but the stallion, fire in its lungs, sought the gap. Only Morgan on Sultan challenged it, and it made the decision to charge.

'Close up on 'em!' Ernie shouted as the rest of the herd galloped right behind the number one mare. She was leading them right in behind her to the waiting trap.

Sultan half reared as he saw the wild stallion thundering towards them, and for the first time Morgan knew a terrible apprehension. Her mind doubted it, yet it was happening. A wild horse was challenging her. It was startling, its destructive aura. There wasn't a single thing she could do but get out of the way. It was a powerful-looking brute and Ty was yelling non-stop for her to clear out.

She wheeled immediately, feeling a wave of panic, and incredibly the wild stallion tracked her in a spectacular territorial display. She had never experienced anything like it. It was not meant to go this way. Now Ty thundered by her, riding straight at the grey stallion. The stallion, momentarily bewildered, turned its attention to breaking the dominion of the big black. No faint-hearted horse, let alone rider, could have faced such a dangerous and unpredictable menace.

There was a roaring in Morgan's ears, her heart turned to stone, but Ty's whip lashed out, forcing the wild stallion to break in its terrible stride. The whole image came close to that of a magnificent wild lion and its fearless tamer. Morgan was to be left with a lasting impression. It burned itself into her brain, so that many years later she shuddered when she remembered that particular morning.

Could she really have done that? No, she couldn't. Accustomed as she was to seeing daily displays of fine horsemanship, she had never seen such daring or acceleration. She took her first real look at her own recklessness. But for Ty, the stallion would have churned her into the ground. He had ridden directly into danger, with never a thought for himself. Literally hurled himself and Lucifer into the front-line with breathtaking courage.

The result of the violent flight of the stallion was that it hurtled into camp like a rocket, so that the men on the ground had to make a frantic run for the trees. The station mare began to scream, hurling herself at the slip rail while the foals huddled for cover. One of the men, one leg stiff from an old injury, turned in fright as the stallion spewed its fury, until Ty, making the only decision he could, dropped the brumby with one shot.

It fell with a heavy thud, and quite extraordinarily the mare stopped her screaming, seemingly bereft of all spirit. She stood to attention, and as Morgan rode into the clearing it was to a stunned and shocked silence.

Morgan looked at Ty miserably. 'Ty, oh, Ty, a thousand thanks!'

He stepped right up to her and pulled her down off her horse. 'It's a short trip to the grave,' he thundered, anger in every inch of his finely tuned body.

She had never seen him so angry. There was an odd pallor beneath his skin and his blue eyes glittered with strange lights. 'What can I say? I'm sorry, I'm *sorry*.' She stood before him, her small face pale and uplifted.

'*Sorry!*' he shouted, and grabbed her.

'Hey, boss!' Ernie Hudson, Jahandra's respected foreman, took one look at Ty's face and risked intervention. On the one hand Morgan's grandfather had stood back and invited her to break her neck, now her cousin was in a fury of fright. Ernie knew which reaction he preferred, but he couldn't stand by and allow little Miss Morgan to come to any harm.

'Out of my way, Ernie,' Ty warned him, a powerhouse of energy and young-man strength.

'What are you gonna do, boss?'

Ty swore. He took a quick look around, then, while the men stood frozen, stunned, he dragged Morgan to a fallen stump, sat on it and pulled her over his knee, administering several short, hard whacks to her small, defenceless rear.

'Spare the rod and spoil the child,' he said. 'You're not brave. You're a lunatic! Pride is a sin!'

Morgan said nothing. She made no movement. She didn't cry out. She took her punishment like a man. She saw now the fear she had inflicted on him. On them all. Every last man looked shocked. Men saw death, wars, but their blood ran cold over women. Protection was their natural role. She saw that now.

'What have you got to say for yourself?' Ty demanded at length. A muscle worked along his jaw and his eyes were the burning blue of the desert sky.

She wanted to beg his forgiveness. Beg all of them to forgive her. Instead she said fierily, 'This isn't going to

look good when we get into court.' Did he really think
she was going to cave in that easily?

'Why, for God's sake, did you do it?' he asked, not
even deigning to acknowledge her remark.

'Seems to me I've done it before.'

Ernie walked up to them, twisting his battered hat
round and round in his hands. 'You must understand
E.J. encouraged her, boss.'

'Don't talk to him, Ernie. I'm here!'

'Beggin' your pardon, miss—you've just given us a
terrible fright.'

'And I'm sorry, Ernie. I'm sorry, all of you.' Morgan
stretched a pleading hand towards the waiting semicircle
of men. 'But we've never had trouble before.'

'Damn it, the stallion was a rogue. You knew it!' Ty
boomed. 'I've tried everything I know with you, to no
avail. We don't need you to hare around like a dare-devil
jackeroo. You've been lucky to reach twenty.'

'OK!' Morgan said stormily. 'You've had your say.
And now we all know you're capable of physical violence. I really don't appreciate being ticked off in front
of the men.'

'Every last one of them has watched you grow up,'
Ty gritted. 'So much for admiring your fearlessness,
you've turned them all grey.'

'I'm no one special,' she countered.

'You're special to them, Morgan. Can't you understand that?'

Ernie sighed. 'That's a fact. Don't like to speak ill of
the dead, but E.J. was one heck of an old bull, so strict
and stern, yet he let you do things no man would allow
his daughter. I got daughters, Miss Morgan, you know
that. They do plenty for their husbands, even tough
things occasionally, but it's the unwritten law that anything dirty or dangerous is for the man!'

'And I'm a droopy, drippy female?' Morgan asked.

'You're not very bright!' Ty said shortly.

Nobody laughed.

Morgan averted her eyes from the fallen stallion. 'Did you have to shoot it?'

'Yes, Morgan, I did,' Ty, the horse-lover, responded curtly. 'I imagine Al might thank me, if you don't.'

'Set to kill me, miss,' Al insisted. 'Probably would have, only the boss moved so fast. You can never trust a wild horse. Never. You oughta remember that.'

'I will, Al,' Morgan promised. 'Sorry to spoil your morning.'

'I'll ride with you, Morgan, as far as the Two Mile,' said Ty.

'My fondest wish is to be on my own.'

Whatever he felt like saying, he spared her. He lifted himself into the saddle while Ernie gave Morgan a leg up.

They rode out of camp in silence, Morgan attempting to hide her confusion. Under his tough veneer, Ty too was shaken. He was the complete opposite of E.J., yet the spark of genius burned brightly in both of them. E.J., for all his faults, and maybe because of them, had built up a mighty pastoral empire. Ty was the fitting guardian. Not only that, Morgan knew in her bones it wouldn't stop there. Ty was committed to achievement. Much as she admired him, and of course she did, it didn't help her. There was no pleasure in being second best. She would never accept it.

'I'm sorry,' he announced suddenly in a voice of extreme impatience.

'You want to talk to me?' she asked haughtily.

'Don't take that tone with me. Once started I mightn't be able to stop. I'm not sorry I turned you over my knee. That was long overdue. I'm sorry I was provoked to the point I did it in front of the men.'

Morgan laughed. 'It's a deep-rooted tradition, isn't it, using physical violence on women?'

'With some women, I'm afraid, there's no alternative,' he returned crisply. 'I practically begged you to give up. I even locked you in your room. How did you get out, by the way?'

'Simple! I climbed over the balustrade and inched along to the big vine. It held me easily. I knew it would.'

'You took a hell of a risk,' he sighed. 'The homestead is in desperate need of repair and restoration. All those millions, and E.J. savoured every cent. How the devil did he get to be so mean?'

'Maybe he was planning on leaving you the richest man in the country.'

He ignored her sarcasm. 'Every man needs a successor. I'm going to need mine.'

'I do hope Camilla has everything in working order.'

'Is that how you hurt your elbow?'

'No problem with my elbow.'

'Ever the little stoic! Do you know what your big problem is, Morgan?'

'Deprivation?' Her eyes flashed.

'E.J. has passed on to you his own warped view of your sex. Instead of being reared a female and rejoicing in it, you're going through life furious you're not a male.'

'May I point out, males get the spoils of this world. I am E.J.'s only grandchild. You rule by divine right. My only role is being companion to you. Your mistress, if you take a mind to it. Let Camilla bear the perfect children, the first-born son your successor. You can balance her dullness with me on the side.'

'Aren't you rather young to be so bitter?' he asked sombrely.

'In fact, I'm not young at all. While you and the twins were doted on by your parents—of course your womenfolk adore you—I survived on school friendships, on the interest and encouragement of my teachers. Fine women with brains. I'm all for developing a woman's brain and spirit. I am a woman, you know.'

'Morgan, you're the most *female* female I know, but you're at war with it. You won't allow yourself to enjoy what you are. I don't like this bitterness. I won't stand around and watch it grow. You have everything in this world going for you. You're beautiful, you're bright, you're perfectly healthy. You're even very rich.'

'But not as rich as you.'

'It's not the money, Morgan.' He silenced her. 'You don't give a damn about money. I know you. It's your feeling of powerlessness. Underneath it all you're still a little lost child. There ought to be laws against allowing a man like E.J. to bring up a child. For God's sakes, don't let him win. Can't you see he tried to rear you in the male role?'

'I'm not a fool.'

'So all this reckless striving is a consequence. You always had to prove yourself. It was criminal. You don't have to prove anything with me. Or anyone else for that matter. You're much admired. Can't you accept that?'

'And that's it in a nutshell, isn't it? A woman has to accept things. Her passivity is much prized.'

'No one could call you passive.'

'You don't have to accept anything, Ty.'

His blue eyes brushed her. 'I can't walk away from you.'

'So there it is. You saved my life again.'

'I didn't think you would really like to die.'

Morgan let her gaze range widely over the luminous plains. 'I want to go with Cecilia and the girls when you fly them to Tyson's Landing.'

'Why? Are you afraid?' He turned his head to look at her.

'I would say I have reason to be.'

'I would never do anything, Morgan, against your will. Not even with your consent, though things are getting kind of torrid. I'll take you back, by all means. Mother will be delighted. Sandra told me you're desperately in

need of new clothes. Why don't you girls fly to Sydney
for a few weeks? Stay at the penthouse. You need a complete break.'

Her lovely mouth down-turned. 'I don't trust you, Ty,
when you're being considerate.'

'On the contrary, trusting me makes you angry. All
this love-hate is scary.'

'I would hardly call it that,' she parried, as coolly as
she could.

'What *would* you call it, Morgan?'

'Rivalry. We're in competition, Ty.'

He laughed, with a genuine note of humour. 'Then
you're about a foot too short. One of these days,
Morgan, you'll come to it. There's great power and
dignity in being a woman. All the satisfaction anyone
could want.'

They flew to Tyson's Landing on the day the flying padre
was due in to conduct a baptism. The baby was the five-
month-old daughter of Bob and Sara Weston. Bob
worked as a stockman, capable and ambitious and
wanting to move up the line. Sara had taken over the
job of cook for the men. All demonstrated their affection by calling off work for the time Padre Luke
Stevens took to conduct the ceremony out in the beautiful
bush setting, using the water from the deep, sparkling
lagoon nearby.

Afterwards the padre preached a short sermon, more
a message of hope, and Morgan and the girls escorted
him back to the homestead where a delicious afternoon
tea was waiting. The padre had developed a wonderful
relationship with his far-flung Outback congregation,
spanning fifty thousand square kilometres and including hundreds of cattle stations and a dozen small
communities and mining settlements. Padre Luke was a
huge man, standing some six feet four, not overweight
but marvellously fit. In manner and appearance he would

have been noticed anywhere, his light-filled blue eyes and his silver head and full beard instantly conjuring up visions of the disciples. He was exceptionally kind, wise and tolerant, but equally well he could subdue the wildest, crudest-mouthed cowhand with a single glance, as he had had to many times. Padre Luke was a household name in the Outback and nothing was more important to him than looking after his flock. He had visited Jahandra countless times, carrying out his ministry, but he had never converted E.J. Neither had he officiated at E.J.'s funeral. The vicar from a distant town had been flown in to do that, but Padre Luke was not offended.

'Of course, E.J. wasn't one of my successes,' he said. 'He never would accept me, even if he never refused me access to the station. One couldn't call him a normal man. He went out of his way to present himself as badly as he could. But I'm not here to judge him. I include him in my prayers.'

It hadn't been E.J. who had contributed to the appeal to buy the padre a new plane, either. Most of the money had been contributed by the Church and the remainder from the community, including a very large donation from the Hartland family of Tyson's Landing.

Morgan found a few moments to talk to the padre alone. She looked on him as a friend, and now she wanted the benefit of his wisdom.

'You've heard of E.J.'s will?' she asked, as they strolled down to feed the black swans in the lagoon.

'And naturally you're upset,' the padre said in his deep, resonant voice.

'Yes,' Morgan acknowledged freely. 'Especially when the main factor has been overlooked. I am E.J.'s only grandchild. Naturally I expected Jahandra at least to myself.'

'And how did you expect to administer it, Morgan?' asked Padre Luke mildly as the swans sailed expectantly towards them.

'I'm an intelligent woman. I've grown up on the job.'

'Well, you certainly impress me. You impress us all but, Morgan, I want you to give this truly objective thought. Running the Hartland empire will be an awesome job. No time off for babies, or rearing them. I know you'll want to marry, and calling to mind your own sad childhood I know you will want to devote yourself to your children. I can see by that small, expressive face that you've taken Ty's elevation over you as a deep personal insult.'

Morgan nodded. 'I even wonder if Ty and E.J. didn't work the whole thing out in private.'

'On the contrary, my dear. I think the whole clan was floored! The hostility between E.J. and Ty was the talk of the Outback. I can promise you Ty had no idea E.J. would arrange things as he did.'

'Then why *did* he, Padre?'

Padre Luke turned to look down on her. 'I don't think it had anything to do with you, or Ty. All E.J. really cared about was the empire he had built up. Badly as he treated Ty, he would have had complete confidence in his ability to take over.'

'Agreed. What you're saying is, he didn't have that same confidence in me.'

'Now, now, my dear. My own view is, E.J. would not have left anything of any importance to any woman, let alone you. No matter how capable or confident you know yourself to be, E.J. was one of that sad breed of men who devalue women. That in itself accounted for a lot of his own unhappiness, and he was an unhappy man, Morgan, for all his overbearing, domineering manner. The thing is he didn't associate power with a woman. Power is for men. You must have known that.'

'Of course I did, but for all the harshness of his be-haviour I never thought for one moment he would leave things this way. Ty has control of Jahandra. He even has half of the homestead.'

'Perhaps the resolution of the problem would be for you two to marry,' Padre Luke suggested jocularly.

'Heavens, Padre, you must understand. Ty and I are totally incompatible.'

He looked at her in astonishment. 'Incompatibility is not what I see. You've been *enjoying* your rivalry all these many years.'

'No, no!' Morgan shook her head.

'Ah, well, eventually you'll see the truth of it. I suspect you're deliberately blinding yourself, Morgan. It's time you abandoned a man's work and started to take pleasure in your feminine nature. The way E.J. reared you has led to some confusion. You've got your norms all mixed up. Sandra mentioned you might fly down to Sydney with them. Knowing you so well, I wouldn't expect you to turn into a social butterfly, but it's only natural to gratify the feminine impulses. You're a beautiful young woman. I'm sure we'd all enjoy seeing you in a dress. No matter who E.J. left the running of his empire to, and obviously he was convinced Ty was the man, very properly he took good care of you. You can accuse him of not giving you outright control, but you cannot accuse him of indifference to your position as his only grand-child. I understand you have been left a very rich young woman. I know, too, you will realise that with great good fortune comes responsibility and service. Whose idea, for instance, was it to find me a new plane?'

'Well, the wings on the old one were just about ready to fall off.'

'Ty. Ty only has to open his mouth and that speeds things up enormously—and he puts money where his mouth is, as you know. E.J. was no great philanthro-pist, but Ty and the family have made many people's lives easier because of their great interest in our far-flung community. There's so much you could do now, my dear. Play a larger part.'

'Cecilia has suggested that. I'm coming round to it.'

'A marvellous woman. And this makes things difficult for her too, Morgan. I understand you're all going back to Jahandra.'

'There's no reason why we won't get on well, yet I understand what you're saying about Cecilia. She'll be giving up her home. I'll be giving up my home as well. I expect when Ty marries we'll all move out. Cecilia has sisters in Sydney. She was always talking about moving closer to them. The twins won't wish to spend their lives on the land. I'm the only one really who'll be displaced.'

'You won't readily adjust to city life, I can see that.'

'I couldn't even build myself something small on Jahandra. When Ty marries, I'll move.'

'I wasn't aware Ty had anyone in mind.'

'What about Camilla Ogilvie?' Morgan burst out.

The padre nodded. 'I've heard about Camilla, of course. I hope she doesn't suffer too keenly, but I don't think Ty will want to spend the rest of his days with her. Strictly between you and me, and repeat it to no one, I think he's already made his decision.'

Morgan was dressing for dinner, trying to make an effort—that remark of the padre's about seeing her in a dress had rankled—when Sandra burst through the door of the adjoining sitting-room.

'Morgan, where are you?'

'Here.' For the first time in her life Morgan felt embarrassed by the inadequacies of her wardrobe. The white dress she wore, though still in good condition, was at least four years old and positively childish, not at all the sort of thing a young woman who cared for herself would wear.

'Guess who's here,' Sandra hissed, rushing to the window and peering out.

'I'm unable to say. Your circle of friends, unlike mine, is very wide.'

'It's Camilla!' Sandra exclaimed with a mighty sigh.

'Oh, how awful!' Morgan's expression signified she felt the same. 'Where did she spring from?'

'She drove over from Clifford Park. She's been staying with the family for a few days. Probably got the idea at the funeral. She's been waiting for us to get home.'

'Would it be all right if I don't come down to dinner?' Morgan asked.

'Of course you've got to come,' Sandra said forcefully. 'But not in that choir dress. You look pathetic. As if you don't belong to us at all.'

'I'm afraid you're right,' Morgan sighed. 'I'd got into the habit of wearing a uniform, day in and day out. E.J. was never much interested in what I wore.'

'I suppose he was unwilling to have a beautiful young woman right under his nose. E.J. was definitely weird. That's what makes it so wonderful Ty is so super. I don't think E.J. really heard about the twentieth century and women's liberation. You can't wear that, Morgan. Camilla will look terrific, as usual.'

'Good for her. I'm not in competition.'

'You can't let the side down, all the same. What a pity you're so short. The rest of us are so much bigger. Come down to my room and we'll try to find something. Maybe you could belt it up, blouse it, something. You might put on a little make-up as well. Your eyes would look enormous with eye-shadow and mascara. I don't understand you at all. Instead of emphasising your assets, you play them down, and even then I promise you you turn every male head. You can't come by that little sexy aura. You're born with it.'

Sandra's large, very feminine bedroom was a study in blue and white, a far cry from Morgan's huge, gloomy bedroom at Jahandra. Once she had asked if she could change the existing Victorian furniture for a beautiful French art nouveau suite in the attic—who had bought it?—but E.J. had turned her down flat. 'Stick to what you've got!' he had told her. For a very rich man E.J. had lived like a miser, which explained Morgan's lifestyle, but Ty's family were long established in the art of living well. The homestead had a warm and welcoming atmosphere. It had been beautifully decorated with many fine pieces, but first and foremost it was a comfortable family home. Sandra's bedroom was enchanting, as was Claire's on the opposite side of the hallway. Morgan had never seen such beautiful fabrics used on curtains and bedspreads and upholstery.

Sandra went to the huge walk-in wardrobe that housed her collection of clothes and accessories. 'Going to have a look?' she asked Morgan, looking back over her shoulder.

'Sure. I was just admiring your taste.'

'Mamma's. Same thing. Claire stole that antique brass bed, you know. It was supposed to be for me. I've got so much that suits my blue eyes, but of course yours are green. I want you to look good. Camilla is such a bitch. It really gets to her, this business between you and Ty.'

'What business?' Morgan marvelled at the racks of clothes.

Sandra paused in her search. 'None of us are too certain just what it is, but there's no question you and Ty spark each other off. Ah, here's something that might do.'

'I suppose so, if I were going down to dinner at the Regent,' Morgan said doubtfully.

'Don't be so silly. You can't stay dreary, you know. You might have worked up an image as a very bright girl, but no one was ever going to ask you where you bought your clothes. Where *did* you buy them, by the way?'

'Absolutely the cheapest place in town. I had to account to E.J. for every penny.'

'Miserable old darling. I suppose I shouldn't talk that way. He remembered us at the end. I suppose it's because we have the same name. Just imagine if you had been Marcia's child by another marriage. He wouldn't have left you a thing. Whew! It doesn't bear thinking about.'

Morgan took the dress. 'This is lovely, Sandra,' she said, holding the brilliantly printed silk dress in front of her, huge hibiscus flowers in green and pink and yellow on a white ground.

'Ungaro,' Sandra said carelessly. 'See how it picks up your eyes. Honestly, I could wrap you in anything. It's really extraordinary, but you remind me of someone out of the Ballet Russe. It's your slanting eyes. Quickly, try it on. You'll have to draw it up some way. A belt on the hips. The rest should be fine. I think Camilla has rather a cheek, turning up like this. I guess her ambitions are making her bold. Do you really think Ty has an interest in her?'

'Well, he told me he ought to be married to her by now.' Morgan's voice was muffled beneath the silk dress.

'He could have been teasing you,' Sandra suggested hopefully.

'I thought you just loved her. You and Claire.'

'Listen, we've come to know her better. She's an appalling snob. I hate that, and she can be really nasty about you. Both Claire and I have told her off along the way. She thinks you're very unusual.'

Morgan shrugged, turning towards the mirror. 'Maybe I am.'

'She says things about Marcia, too,' Sandra growled.

'Marcia?' Morgan turned in amazement. 'Why would she want to pick on Marcia? I doubt if she's laid eyes on my frivolous mother more than two or three times in her life.'

'Well, Marcia is an eyeful, you must admit. Too bad she's such a bad mother. Mamma says at the outset she was perfectly all right, but E.J. overpowered her, as he did everyone else. Probably after your father died she couldn't make the effort to fight him. There was no one better than E.J. at putting a woman down, which is why we're all so proud of you.'

'This is news!' Morgan turned as though she couldn't believe what she was hearing. 'You're proud of me?'

Sandra nodded. 'The fact is, we were desperately unhappy E.J. cut you off from the rest of us. Mamma had some frightening confrontations with him. All for you. Didn't do a bit of good. In fact, Mamma actually stopped because not only was she making no impression, E.J. tightened up. Extraordinary what lies inside people. No wonder authors have no end of stories. There seems to be a drama in every family. Turn around, Morgan. I don't think you need do anything but gather it in to your waist. It's a bit long, but it suits you. You positively cannot wear those shoes.'

'I'll have to.'

'Maybe I can colour change them.' Sandra nibbled on her lip. 'You could look positively enchanting if you tried. Even in your terrible clothes, you have a certain style.'

'All those ballet lessons.' Morgan smiled. 'E.J. was selective about how he spent his money. Maybe he thought he would benefit by making me stronger. I went backwards after Marcia left me. All children are attached to their mothers, no matter what the maternal instinct.'

'But you sought her out?' Sandra sat back on the bed, looking at Morgan with sympathetic eyes.

'Wouldn't you?'

'I thank God every day for my mother,' Sandra said simply. 'If I had had to endure your life, heavens knows what I would have developed into. You have a marvellous capacity for fighting back. At the same time, I think you're fighting the wrong person. In the normal course of events women don't take over huge ventures. I'm not saying they can't, but surely we women derive our greatest pleasure and satisfaction from the natural female role? Almost all of us want family: a husband, children, running our own home. Some choose careers as all-important, but at some time they must wonder if they've made the right decision. Let's face it, Morgan, running what took more than one hundred years to build up won't be easy. Men care about business in a different way from women. What's a pleasure to Ty might prove a real headache for you. Don't make power the central part of your life.'

'I don't care about power, Sandy.'

'I think you do. Your upbringing directed you towards it.'

'Then E.J. cut me down.'

'To size.' Sandra smiled. 'What now, Morgan? E.J. made his decision. You can do nothing to change it. I understand your feelings of helpless rage.'

'I don't think you do, Sandy. There's a marked difference between me and you and Claire.'

'There's not the difference you'd like to believe. Let's look at our main aim in life. I want to be loved. Do you?'

'Of course.' Morgan's tone was intense.

'Emotions are what is important. They make us happy or they make us suffer. Look at E.J.! He was one of the richest men in the country, yet happiness passed him by. What you really want is softening up. Won't you come to Sydney with us? Don't feel you have to do anything you don't want to. I know you don't like the party scene, but sometimes you've had fun. We'll choose carefully where we go, and you're desperately in need of clothes. Don't you really want to enhance your appearance?'

Morgan smiled wryly. 'Now that you call attention to it, I do. I couldn't do much, you know, when E.J. was alive. He didn't like to see me wearing make-up, so there was no sense in subjecting myself to additional censure. I can see how good I look in this dress.'

'You'll look better with a little make-up,' said Sandra. 'I can't offer you foundation. We're all very fair and you're olive. But I've got everything else. You have a beautiful skin, in any case. I never can tan.'

Someone knocked on the door behind them, then Claire entered, a vision in a lapis blue evening shirt, with padded shoulders, and matching trousers.

'Boy, have we got a problem,' she said.

Sandra nodded. 'Camilla's here.'

'You have to come and do something! Mamma is being charming, but I know she's annoyed. You would think Camilla would let us know, instead of turning up on the doorstep.'

'Where's Ty?'

'He's not in yet. There are so many things that have to be discussed. The stakes are very high for Camilla now. I'm sure if she could she'd throw a lasso around Ty...'

'The question is, does he care about her?' Sandra asked. 'Morgan said he told her he should be married to Camilla by now.'

'Go on, Morgan,' Claire invited, taking a deep breath.

'Nothing to go on about. He simply made that remark.'

'How shocking!' Claire plonked down beside her twin.

Morgan studied them for a moment, admiring the golden aura that surrounded them. The beautiful Hartland twins. Now they looked most disturbed. 'I must say, I thought you two were one hundred per cent for Camilla.'

'I told you, all that has changed. We've come to see what Camilla is really like. She's all over us, and I'll have to admit we were blinded by it, but we've had plenty of opportunity to observe her manner with those less fortunate.'

'She speaks about you, too, Morgan,' Claire said angrily. 'For a long time now she has spoken as though she's in competition with you over Ty. What I'm really trying to say is, she's jealous.'

'For God's sake, what brought on these feelings?' Morgan's green eyes flared. 'It doesn't exactly make sense. Ty and I are more likely to fight than anything else.'

'But it's strong emotion, Morgan,' Sandra told her. 'You may not realise this, but everyone else does. Both of you are more intense talking to each other than at any other time. Ty only has to say the least little thing and you respond at once. His natural tendency is to curb your real recklessness. I know he worries about you. That feeling, the anxiety and the caring, Camilla hates. She sees you as a real force in Ty's life, and why not? Something binds you.'

'Because we're family.'

'If that were all, why isn't he the same way with Lucinda and Helen? They're Hartlands, too.'

'I think his relationship with E.J. played a part in it. Ty has a very protective streak. You obey him out of love and respect. He arouses a whole lot of conflict in me.'

'Trust him,' Claire said. 'That's very important. He controls all our lives. Don't you think it a miracle he's motivated by love? Ty would never hurt you, Morgan, just as he would never hurt us. Such a thing is unthinkable. You grew up trying to copy Ty.'

'*What?*'

'Don't you think you did?' Claire wavered at Morgan's sharp, shocked tone.

'I've never for one moment considered it.'

'Consider it now. I would say some conflict is inevitable. Unless you come to terms with being a woman, your self-esteem will always be threatened. In a sense, we've all been dominated by E.J. and Ty. We could never win. Not in any real sense. It's understood the man is the symbol of power. E.J. and Ty were like two giants facing each other. I think men are fearful at times. They need women to give them balance. To make them better people. E.J. had no woman in his life, more's the pity. He just got harder and harder, and eventually we all rejected him. I'm sure if he'd been happily married he would have acted differently. As it was, he was the arch-type of a tyrant.'

'Not that it matters now,' Sandra sighed. 'What do you think of that dress on Morgan?'

'Great!' Claire inspected Morgan's slight, petite figure from head to toe. 'The shoes will have to go.'

'I think I can do something about them,' Sandra said. 'Morgan is considering coming to Sydney with us.'

'Oh, do come, Morgan,' Claire urged. 'You have to move beyond this restricted life. Personally, I think you need total change for a while. All you've ever done is work, work, work. How you've never seriously injured yourself I'll never know.'

'How long is Camilla staying?' Sandra asked. 'Did she say?'

'Doubtless she'll tell us in her own time. Mamma put her in the bedroom above the landing. It's the most glamorous, after all, and far enough away from us all. Don't tell her we intend to go to Sydney. She'll be over at Jahandra like a flash. You know if Ty decided to marry her there's absolutely nothing we could do.'

'There's something I could do,' Morgan said fierily. 'There's no way I'm going to share my home with Camilla Ogilvie. Pushy as she is, she'll never get the best of me. Ty will have to consider someone entirely different if he wants any peace.'

'Hear, hear!' said the twins.

CHAPTER FIVE

CAMILLA was charming. Her conversation was honeyed and entirely without sting. She was as tall as the twins, ultra slim but strongly boned, with a shoulder-length bronze mane and a fire in her golden-brown eyes. Like the twins, she dressed beautifully at all times and she had the same polished aura money ensured. But, whereas the twins were very relaxed and confident in their manner, Camilla's confidence veered towards arrogance. Mercifully it was not in evidence that evening. When she put her mind to it Camilla Ogilvie could be excellent company. She was well educated and much travelled. Her family had a secure position in society, but outside her own circle Camilla's dyed-in-the-wool snobbery did her no credit. Only certain people in her view were born to inherit the earth, and she had no wish to make the acquaintance of the rest.

Ty appeared to be relishing her company. Her golden-brown gaze was very frank and direct. It was obvious she found him attractive, the whole package spiced by his overnight rise to great wealth and power. Dinner passed very pleasantly, a grand affair in Morgan's experience. E.J. liked to be silent at dinner. They had never done anything so cosy or informal as dining in the morning-room, much less the kitchen. They used the formal dining-room under a great glittering chandelier, E.J. at one end, Morgan miles away at the other. It had been her private joke to hold conversation with herself, but there was nothing like that tonight. There was much laughter and talk. The table looked superb. Beautiful ivory linen place mats and napkins, heavily laced and scalloped around the edges, Wedgwood dinnerware, ornate silver, the sparkle of Waterford crystal, single white roses in tall slender vases along the length of the table and the romance of candle flames reflected in the tall giltwood mirrors that hung above the sideboard and the white marble fireplace. It was a far cry from dinner at Jahandra, a deadly dull meal for as far back as Morgan could remember.

'What are you thinking about, Morgan?' Camilla asked lightly. 'You've gone very quiet.'

'I was thinking how lovely everything is.' Morgan's great eyes were, for once, very soft and misty. 'It occurred to me I've developed no great talent for living.'

'My dear, you weren't given the opportunity, that's all.' Cecilia, in shimmering blue, smiled at her. 'You have a great sense of beauty. I, too, was watching your face.'

'My grandfather took all the fun out of life, didn't he?'

'He certainly did!' Camilla seconded and laughed. 'It will be a real challenge for Ty's wife to turn that immense shrine into something charming and livable in. All that heavily carved Victorian furniture, drapes and cushions that look as if they'd turn to dust. It's a colossal place really for these days. I always found it incredibly intimidating, especially when I happened to encounter E.J. on the main stairway. He was so grim, yet dignified in a remote way. Essentially a warrior prince. Someone royal, anyway. There was that aura of isolation. Whatever woman handles the restoration, she will have to have a marvellous sense of scale and colour. The place is so gloomy.'

'Cecilia and I will be doing it up,' Morgan announced, totally unaware of her own regal air.

'Really?' Camilla lost her smile. 'You wouldn't wait for Ty's wife?'

'As far as I know, Ty hasn't found one. In any case, Jahandra is mine too. If I'm not up to running a mighty pastoral empire, I am up to refurbishing the mausoleum I've lived in all my life.'

'But surely you won't always live there?' Camilla asked, the golden bronze of her dress reflecting her glittering eyes.

'Oh, I expect so,' Morgan said lightly. 'As you said, it's a huge house. There's a good deal of room. One could live there for years without passing on the stairs.'

The first cracks began to appear. 'I expect Ty's future wife might be a bit upset about that,' Camilla suggested rather acidly.

'Oh, I hope not,' Morgan replied. 'I only want to love her.'

'What do you think, Ty?' Camilla asked.

'It's as much Morgan's house as mine.' He glanced at Morgan sidelong.

'Well...' Camilla hesitated. 'You know what they say. You can't have two women under the one roof.'

'There are going to be *four* of us shortly,' Sandra pointed out sweetly. 'I say that's a good idea doing up the house, Morgan.'

'Cecilia, you must help me.'

'I'd love to, Morgan,' Cecilia said, meaning it. 'Even so, I feel we need a certain amount of professional help. Jahandra is a palace compared to this. I've known the dining-room to seat a hundred people. It would be an enormous task, yet I know we would get great pleasure from it. The colours for the interior painting alone will present quite a challenge. Clearly we need expert advice, and I know just the firm to provide it. They advise on all the major houses.'

'The garden needs professional attention as well. I've always wanted to develop new areas. We need a landscape artist to help us.'

'There's a danger Ty's wife might not like what you do,' Camilla insisted.

Morgan was unhesitating. 'If the worst comes to the worst, and Ty marries someone who isn't easily pleased, he'll have to build somewhere else on the property. There are endless sites.'

'Is that so?' Ty drawled negligently.

'You're joking, of course, Morgan.' Camilla tried to smile.

'Well, *you* wouldn't want to move in with me, would you?' Morgan's face lit with humour.

'I certainly would not,' Camilla responded, disconcerted. 'It's quite possible you'll marry in the near future yourself. You would have a problem persuading a husband to stay on Jahandra.'

'Someone like Pat O'Donough would move in tomorrow.'

'Ah!' Camilla said in a sly voice. 'Is that the way the wind blows? I've heard rumours, of course.'

'Then we ought to sue for slander,' Ty laughed briefly. 'Morgan has no interest in O'Donough whatever!'

'Of course I have,' Morgan said.

'Shall we have coffee in the other room?' Cecilia suggested. 'Perhaps out on the veranda. The sky is brilliant tonight. There's no magic like an Outback night sky. One could almost reach out and capture a star.'

Afterwards Camilla caught Ty by the arm and drew him down into the garden for a walk, and while Cecilia and the twins organised what they wanted to take back to Jahandra, Morgan drifted into the music-room and opened up the Steinway. The twins had taken piano lessons at school and developed a pleasing talent. Morgan had real ability. Even E.J. had taken the time to listen to her play. Whatever he paid for she had to excel at, but even then he had never bought her a beautiful grand piano like this.

She sat down and let her fingers move over the keys. She had not been practising of late, with so little time available to her, but now she had all the time in the world.

The opening bars of a Chopin ballade spilled into the room, the beautiful sound reduced by having the lid down. Morgan stood up and carefully removed a beautiful flower lamp, art deco in design, and three silver-framed photographs of the family: one of Ty looking stunningly handsome, one of the twins in evening dress, another of the twins with their mother. All of them looked perfectly beautiful. Cecilia was a wonderful mother. She had brought great love and joy into her children's lives. Morgan, too, had a desire for children, and she would live up to the maternal role. Marcia had only pretended to be a mother. Was it any wonder that, so abandoned, Morgan had not yet arrived at a true sense of identity?

Once she started to play, Morgan forgot everything but the music and the deep emotions within her. The music floated out into the night, contemplative and turbulent by turns. Her young fingers had lost none of their dexterity and the circumstances of her life had lent her a unique insight into the depths of the human soul. She played with great feeling and understanding, so Cecilia broke off her tasks to sit out on the veranda to listen and the twins walked to and fro, completely enchanted.

Only Camilla was uninspired by the impromptu concert. When they returned to the house twenty minutes later, Ty started towards the music-room and Camilla was compelled to follow him. Morgan, totally immersed, was only half-way through a Brahms intermezzo, but Camilla clapped wildly.

'Bravo, bravissimo!'

Morgan jumped, a little startled, and turned. 'Oh, you're back!' Her green eyes were strangely unfocused.

'You really have such a powerful touch for a woman,' Camilla carolled. 'I'm sure I couldn't get that amount of sound from a piano.'

'But then, you don't have Morgan's gift,' said Ty.

'I know. Dramatic! One doesn't expect it from such a little thing. You must have had a concert pianist in the family closet.'

'Not that we know of.' Morgan went to get up, but Ty stopped her.

'Don't stop. The whole station is listening.'

Morgan shook her head, knowing full well Camilla's dismay. 'I'm very much out of practice.'

'It didn't sound like that to me.'

'Oh, leave her, Ty. I'm sure the poor girl's tired.'

'Not at all, but I offered to help Cecilia.'

Camilla's golden-brown eyes gleamed. 'What you really ought to do with Jahandra homestead is convert it into *two* houses.'

'Never!' Ty said with extreme distaste.

'You don't think it a gamble to move in together?'

'We get on very well.' Ty let his glance rest on Morgan's triangular face.

'You could have fooled me,' Camilla laughed. 'You and Morgan are always at loggerheads.'

'Would you rather we didn't have the family?' Morgan asked.

'What an extraordinary will!' Camilla evaded, though her slim body gave a definite frisson. 'Chaining you together in this way. It simply won't work. Each of you will very soon want to be without the other.'

'We'll get through,' said Ty lightly.

Camilla's eyes flickered. 'I'm not so sure.'

'Morgan and I have to make a great many decisions together. We could even have to live together permanently,' said Ty, and he gave a playful, anguished groan.

'You're teasing, Ty,' Camilla said, brightening. 'That's the craziest thing I've ever heard!'

'Bless you.' His blue eyes sparkled.

'Morgan *is* quite attractive,' Camilla considered, bronze head on one side. 'It won't be very long before someone sweeps her off her feet. You ought to consider that before you start redecorating the house, Morgan. Surely that will be the right of Ty's wife? After all, he is the one who will remain on Jahandra.'

'I have to keep reminding myself of that,' said Morgan. 'Nevertheless, I've lived far too long in a way I didn't want. I think we'll do a great job of refurbishing Jahandra. For all I know Ty mightn't get married for years yet. I think forty is a nice age. By then a man should know his own mind.'

Camilla was suddenly gripped by something that looked like panic. 'You're far too attached to Ty, you know.'

'I agree.' Morgan was startled by her own admission. 'But then, he has always been in my life. Excuse me now, won't you? There's so much to do if we have to meet our schedule.'

Camilla was not to be deterred. She cornered Morgan before breakfast the next morning and asked her to take a walk down to the lagoon.

'Of course, you know the situation between Ty and me,' she said shortly, reaching out and breaking off a pink bauhinia blossom.

'You had better tell me.' Morgan raised her eyes.

Camilla laughed suddenly. 'You know perfectly well. What an odd little creature you are!'

'You obviously like to think so.'

'I mean, who are you like?'

Morgan allowed herself a wry smile. 'Probably someone on my mother's side of the family.'

'Ah, yes, Lady Ainsley. You're not really your mother, either.'

'No. It's an eye-opener all right.'

'I'm afraid it is,' Camilla returned tartly. 'Extraordinary, when you think about it.'

Morgan turned to look at her. 'It's such a beautiful morning, Camilla. I'll have to run if you're going to be difficult.'

'Not before you hear me out.' Camilla discarded the butterfly bauhinia.

'I can't imagine what it is you have to say.'

'Plenty.' Camilla's bronze eyes looked angry. 'This inter-relation between you and Ty I'm finding obstructive. You're perfectly well aware Ty and I are much more than friends.'

'I had no idea. Absolutely none!' Morgan lied.

Camilla was aquiver with frustration. 'I do wish you wouldn't joke. I had hoped to speak some sense.'

'That's sweet of you, Camilla, and I appreciate it. Do go on about you and Ty.'

Camilla snorted. 'We've discussed marriage,' she said in a clipped voice.

'And when was that?'

'You don't have to know. Just believe what I'm telling you.'

'Why should I? You could be making it up.' Morgan purposely looked down to check her watch.

'You're a very strange girl,' Camilla told her.

'Right now, I think you're the one who's strange. There's something you ought to know about me, Camilla. When someone tries to get at me I usually tell them to get lost. Please excuse the plain speaking, but that's the way I am. I grew up under E.J. It's extremely unlikely I'd be intimidated by someone like you.'

Camilla flushed and backed away. 'Don't you think you're over-reacting?'

'Doubtful. You've told me twice I'm strange. You've also commented I'm like no one in the family. You don't appreciate the —inter-relation, was it?—between Ty and me. Is there anything else?'

'Well, surely you can understand the position I'm in?' Camilla queried.

'No, I don't. So far it's all a jumble.'

'Ty and I would have been married long ago, but for you.'

'A little more of us,' Morgan said, 'and I'll screech. What have I to do with the two of you?'

Camilla now picked up a pebble and pitched it at the ducks. 'Ty feels he has to look after you. It's worse now that E.J. has gone.'

'Leave the ducks alone. God forgive me for saying it, but it's a whole lot better without E.J. If you're trying to confuse me, Camilla, you're doing a great job. If Ty wants to marry you, he will.'

'You come first!' Camilla cried wrathfully.

Morgan thought about it. 'That's nonsense.'

'No, it's not, and I can't live with it. I see you as the one person who stands between us.'

'Because we share an inheritance?'

'You're too close.'

Morgan took a deep breath of the warm, shimmering air. 'What would you have me do? Move out of my own home?'

'Why not?' Camilla asked as if it were perfectly reasonable. 'You have all the money you could possibly want. Why do you want to be stuck out here when you could travel the world? You could meet people. You could let yourself acquire some sophistication. You seem to impress a lot of people, but all in all you've got a lot to learn. You've already taken up too much of Ty's time. Why don't you go and find a man of your own?'

'If it's any business of yours, I plan to,' Morgan told her. 'When I'm good and ready. What did you hope to gain by this little chat?'

'Just a shade more co-operation.' Camilla laughed shortly. 'You don't appear to know when you're not wanted.'

Morgan shrugged. 'You're the expert! You're working too hard, Camilla. Leave it to Ty. I really don't appreciate getting this kind of flak, either. We're all Hartlands. You're the outsider, and let's face it, it could very easily stay that way.'

Camilla turned to stare at her, full mouth working. 'You're my enemy, aren't you?'

Morgan returned her gaze steadily. 'You're making it difficult for me to like you, but I certainly don't hate you. The thing is, Camilla, I don't give a damn about you. Ty can marry whomever he likes. I think I'm big-hearted enough to take it. I didn't want things this way, you know. I fully expected Jahandra to be mine!'

'And how is that?' Camilla sneered. 'I couldn't see a man like Edward Hartland leaving the control of his entire holdings to little more than a child.'

'I still say he should have, but never mind. You're welcome to visit Jahandra whenever you like. I'll keep out of the way somehow. But I'm not taking off just to please you. Whatever progress you think you've made with Ty, let me tell you, as one who knows, he's a hard man to follow.'

'I love him,' Camilla said.

'Most women are dumb. About men.'

'Maybe you love him too,' Camilla suggested angrily.

'Actually, he makes me madder than anyone else I know. I don't know if that's love.'

Camilla picked up another pebble, this time hurling it far out into the lagoon. 'Sooner or later you'll have to go,' she pointed out. 'You couldn't be cruel enough to stay around and ruin some woman's life.'

'You mean when Ty's married?' Morgan asked.

'It would be very upsetting to have to vie for Ty's attention.'

'That doesn't apply to me,' Morgan said briefly. 'Ty's attention is more of a hassle. I'm not trying to divide you, Camilla. Heaven help me, I haven't even thought of it. Everyone notices the effect Ty and I have on one another. It's one of those things no one can explain. We can't do anything about it, either. As E.J.'s heirs we're tied together. The woman Ty marries will have to get used to that. I've been a victim all my life, Camilla, but not any more. I'm new to power, but I'll get around to using it. I hope, wisely. One thing I won't do is give up what's mine. I believe I have the moral right to ask Ty to build his wife another home when the time comes. It should be simple on a million acres. Jahandra is part of me. It's in my blood. I won't let go.'

'It's impossible!' Camilla exploded.

'Why don't you talk about it to Ty?' Morgan suggested wearily.

'I'll never accept you, Morgan. *Never.*'

'Then be careful you don't ruin your chances,' Morgan warned her.

Morgan tried to forget her exchange with Camilla as she rode around Tyson's Landing, but it was impossible. It was a fantastic situation they were now all in. She couldn't bear to think about Ty with a wife. There were too many difficulties there, conflicts she was unwilling to face. Ty's lovemaking was like physical pain, commanding all her attention. Her relationship with him had always had its roots in attraction. The outward display of it she had abruptly withdrawn the summer she turned thirteen. What she felt for Ty was like a fatal disease. She would never be free of it until she died.

Camilla did have a legitimate point. No young woman, newly married, could expect to be happy knowing that she was going to share her home and her husband with another woman. What E.J. had done was sit them all on a powder-keg. Of course she could withdraw and forfeit her share of the homestead to Ty. Women were expected to do things like that since time immemorial. But Morgan felt more like putting up a real fight. How could she explain to anyone apart from Ty what the land meant to her? What *Jahandra* meant to her. Its hold on her was invincible. She could enjoy the cities for a time but, unlike the twins, she couldn't continue to exist happily there. It was the Outback that spoke to her; the spirit of the glowing red desert. Even Tyson's Landing, hundreds of miles to the north-east, shining emerald green under the tropical sun, was less sacred to her. Nothing in Morgan's eye could equal the powerful, poignant grandeur of the Channel Country. Either one was totally absorbed by it, or it was a profoundly strange and lonely place. Morgan loved it like one of the ancients. She had been fully initiated long ago.

Ty found her with the men as they took a break from the morning muster. He collected a steaming mug of billy tea and joined her where she was resting under the glorious canopy of a flowering acacia.

'Steven will be joining us Wednesday,' he told her, lowering his lithe, elegant body to the ground. 'Needless to say he and Susan are thrilled with the change-over.'

'As well they might be,' Morgan observed. 'Apart from the homestead being a wonderful place to live, this is a big step up the ladder for him.'

Her slight sarcasm had no visible effect on Ty. 'Steven's a good man, Morgan. You know that. We need family. People we can trust. Steven and Sue can be depended upon to do the job well. I wouldn't put just anyone into the homestead. My mother looks on it as her home. The place she grew up. All she has left of her parents. Like you, she cherishes the land. Perhaps not so exclusively or so passionately, but Tyson's Landing means a very great deal to her. Sue was born to our sort of life. She'll know how to look after everything.'

'Yes.' Liking Sue as she did, Morgan could scarcely disagree. 'The one who's unhappy around here is your girlfriend.'

'She's in Melbourne this week.' Ty narrowed his eyes against the rising hot vapour.

'Not Kerri Lockhart.' Morgan glanced coolly at him. 'The one who's been around the longest. Why don't you do Camilla a favour and give her a straight answer?'

'To what? I've forgotten,' he replied smoothly.

'According to her you've discussed marriage. According to you you should have been married to her by now. Doesn't that say something?'

'If it makes you feel any better I've never discussed marriage with Camilla. Various girls have crossed my mind from time to time. Camilla was a definite possibility, but in the end, I had to cross her off the list. Haven't you noticed what a bitch she can be? It's an education to hear her order the station staff about. *Our* station staff. I think they'd all take off if Camilla ever got control. She treats everyone not in her swish circle like dirt.'

Morgan nodded. 'Even so, you appear to enjoy her company. She's so ambitious you might be able to persuade her to adopt a less blatantly arrogant style. I think it's a permanent personality trait myself, but you never know.'

'Has Camilla been at you?' he asked.

'What's it worth to pass on the information?' Morgan set her empty mug down.

'A chance to be alone together,' he suggested, drily.

'Forget it.'

'I take it she's upset you in some way.'

Morgan sighed and leant her raven head back against the soft grey tree-trunk. 'My thoughts keep returning to a few things she said. Splitting the homestead between us has created many problems. Not the least, uprooting Cecilia. The twins don't seem to care. They're mad to get to Sydney in any case. You *will* marry and I can't see your wife accepting me.'

'Then I'll be forced to remain a bachelor,' said Ty promptly.

'Nonsense!' Morgan snapped. 'I couldn't count the number of women after you, and what about your successor?'

'That *is* a serious concern,' Ty agreed lazily, his eyes on her profile and the swan-like column of her neck. 'Why don't we face this problem when it arises?'

'Because it could arise tomorrow!' Morgan sat up and gave him a disgusted stare. 'It's all up to me, isn't it? I have to do the decent thing and move out. In the overall situation, I'm the expendable one. You must remain. I imagine, like Camilla, very many women would be put off by the idea of sharing their home with another woman. In a real sense I wasn't left half of Jahandra at all. Pressures are already mounting to get me out.'

'Have I asked you?' Ty questioned.

'The point is, you're so one-track you could well expect someone like Camilla to accept a near-impossible situation. I'm not even *elderly*.'

'You sure ain't!' Ty drawled. 'Did I tell you you looked beautiful in Sandy's dress? I always knew you could look like that. I'll admit it would be risky having you around. More like having your own enchantress on the scene, but I know what Jahandra means to you. I would never ask you to live anywhere else.'

'You might if you fell in love.' She dipped her head.

'Are you telling me you think I don't know what love's like?'

'Do you?' She turned to stare into his azure eyes.

'Beyond your experience, elf.'

She looked away and shook her head, almost dissolving at his tone. 'What's to become of us, Ty?'

'Leave it to me,' he said simply.

'That's easy for a lot of people, but not for me.'

'Let's ride,' he said, abruptly, standing up and extending his hand. Everything about him was bold, superbly self-assured. 'You'll be twenty-one in just over ten weeks' time. You haven't asked for it and probably would never get around to it, but I'm giving you a big party.'

Morgan was conscious of both pleasure and shock. 'Surely not! We've only just buried E.J.'

Ty looked down his straight nose. 'E.J. had his say for the past fifty years. Three months is a fair time. Anyway, I'm far more concerned with you than a false mourning for E.J. He tried to conceal you from the world. I intend to show you off.'

Sydney was a world away, a great cosmopolitan city blessed with the most glorious harbour in the world, magnificent beaches, long hot summers for water sports, endless space, freedom and entertainments, and for Morgan an incredible world of shopping.

The twins ran her off her feet, thrilled to be outfitting her as her position demanded. Morgan went along with it all, determined to enjoy her stay. The penthouse overlooked a brilliant turquoise bay, picturesquely dotted with a flotilla of expensive yachts, and each morning they had their breakfast on the plant and flower-filled terrace, planning what they would do with the time.

'Say you'll come to the party tonight,' Sandra begged her. 'Rick said he'll call for us.'

'I'm off to Marcia's.' Morgan surprised them.

'Did she really invite you?' Claire asked sardonically.

'I invited myself. Not that she didn't ask when I said I was in Sydney for a few weeks. She wants to see you girls, of course. She suggested we all meet for lunch, but there are a few things I have to ask her on my own.'

'Such as?' Claire bit into a freshly baked croissant.

'You could call it private.'

'I've a feeling you're up to something, Morgan.'

Morgan ignored that. 'Why don't we take a day trip on the harbour? It's all terribly familiar to you, but not to me. It's a perfect day. Look at the water and the sky!'

'Rick is taking us out on his yacht at the weekend,' said Claire.

'No let's go today,' Sandra urged her twin. 'It's Morgan's holiday, after all. You've no idea how happy I am we're all together. I wonder if Graham is going to send you more flowers today.' She gave Morgan a teasing look. 'Carnations, Monday. Roses, Tuesday. Orchids, Wednesday.'

'He's wasting his time.' Claire threw back her blonde head and laughed. 'He only met you Saturday. Now he's crazy for you. Allow us to take a little of the credit. You certainly pay for dressing. What's it like to be compared to—what was it, a flawless flower?'

'How did I have that effect, anyway?' Morgan asked carelessly, her eyes on the dipping yachts.

'Half your luck!' Claire moaned. 'Graham Ellis is considered quite a catch. Someone told me he's outstanding at corporate law.'

'I'm sure we could use him,' Morgan said mildly. If only Ty were here, she thought. *Ty. Ty.* She had the hollow feeling she was going to be haunted by him all her life.

They had a very happy day out on the harbour, enjoying the company of three Japanese girls, tourists who spoke excellent English and were at the start of an Australian tour which would eventually bring them to the Outback. Of course they were invited to stay at Jahandra if they found themselves in the general area, and names and addresses were exchanged. All the girls were university graduates and this was the year their parents had allotted them to see something of the world. Australia had been a long-time fascination for them and they were astounded at the amount of space. Morgan thought it would take them a very long time to relate to the immensity of the interior. They had a wide range of *musts* and all were determined to nurse a koala. It was international exchange at its best. A stranger might have thought they were all lifelong friends.

The twins went off to their party and at seven thirty on the dot Morgan slipped into the back seat of her step-father's Rolls. It was only a short drive to the Ainsley harbourside mansion. Marcia had told her they would be dining alone. Philip had a previous engagement confirmed weeks ago.

Marcia came down the stairway as a maid let Morgan in the door. At a slight distance she looked no more than twenty-five, at close range early thirties. She was in fact ten years older, but diet and the best of care kept her lavish good looks almost unimpaired. Marcia was petite like Morgan, very feminine, and a certain resemblance linked them, more of body type and grace of movement, and occasional-fleeting expressions.

'Ah, darling!' Marcia's lovely face lit up as she took in Morgan's polished appearance. 'How charming you look!' She allowed Morgan to peck her cheek, taking hold of her daughter's hands and inspecting her as though she were a model on parade. 'The twins have been at work on you, I see.'

'I think we've bought out half Sydney,' Morgan agreed lightly.

'Good. Good.' Marcia looked genuinely pleased. 'It's high time you started to capitalise on what you've got. The Hartlands are beautiful girls, of course, but they haven't got what you've got! You look perfect. Quite French. I'm so sorry Philip isn't here. He'd be so pleased to see you looking this way. You always did look less than your best when that old tyrant was alive. Come into the drawing-room, darling. We'll have a pre-dinner drink before Heaton calls us.'

'You look wonderful, Marcia, as ever.' Morgan followed her mother into the white and gold drawing-room. Marcia always had been fond of a lot of gilt.

'I wanted this to be very light and sunny,' Marcia explained, waving a small, enamel-tipped hand.

'You've certainly achieved your aim.' Morgan sat down in a very elegant Empire chair, painted white and gold and covered with white and gold embroidered silk. The floor was white marble, the walls a deep yellow moiré, the paintings neo-classical; there were gilded side-tables, two marvellous chandeliers, white and gold over-mantel and two gold and white winged creatures holding up a marble console. It was a very imposing, formal room and Morgan didn't like it. It looked as though no one had ever sat there before now.

Marcia, not perturbed or offended by Morgan's obvious wish to sit alone, sank down on a delightful curving sofa upholstered in the same yellow moiré as the walls. She wore her favourite white—'White is such a flattering colour'—turning a bland face to her daughter. 'I'm so sorry, darling, we couldn't be with you for E.J.'s funeral.'

'Please, Marcia,' Morgan gave a little laugh, 'you don't have to pretend with me. You hated E.J. and even I've stopped crying. Death is such a terrible thing. I cried because he was such a lost, tragic man.'

'E.J.—tragic?' Marcia's delicate arching brows shot up in massive disbelief.

'How could he ever have felt good about himself?' Morgan asked. 'Don't you think it tragic to live a life without love?'

'Darling, I have *Philip*!'

'Whom you've never loved.'

Marcia sighed deeply. 'Such a difficult girl you are, darling. You look marvellous. Please don't depress me.'

'Have you ever loved anyone, Marcia?' Morgan asked, feeling so crowded by doubts that she persisted.

'Darling, how stupid! I loved your father.'

'You never seemed to suffer when you lost him.'

'Oh, wake up!' Marcia apparently couldn't bear her daughter's searching eyes because she jumped up and walked to one of the tall, arching windows that led out on to the wide terrace. 'You were only a child.'

'You can justify anything. So many people lately have spoken of my looks. How strange it is that I don't resemble anyone in the family.'

Marcia whirled, her chiffon skirt flaring. 'Is there something wrong, really, because you're not a blue-eyed blonde? Take it from me, you're the *image* of my mother!'

'Am I really?'

Marcia frowned, perturbed by the gravity of Morgan's expression. 'What on earth is all this about, Morgan?' Her smoky-grey gaze was intense and angry. 'I wish I had photos to show you, but unfortunately I haven't.'

'Isn't that just a bit odd? Most people have a photograph or two?'

'Are you doubting my word?' Marcia challenged.

'Why are you always on the run from me, Marcia? Sit down.'

Marcia did so, her porcelain cheeks flushing. 'Easy to see that old autocrat reared you. *Sit down.* How dare you give me orders in my own home?'

'I have a few rights, Mother. There's a lot of unfinished business between you and me.'

Marcia's face suddenly crumpled and she looked her age. 'I was feeling really good about this evening, Morgan. How *could* you?'

Morgan demonstrated her seriousness by pushing on. 'Why have you always created these barriers, Marcia? Kept me at such a distance?'

'Because E.J. wanted it,' Marcia cried desperately.

'How can a mother withdraw her love? I know I would never lose my child.'

'You know nothing about life yet, Morgan,' Marcia said flatly. 'Being very rich is a great start. No one can hold power over you for long. When I married your father I had just got over a very bad affair. I was alone.

I had *nothing*. Your father came along and I saw my chance. Under normal circumstances I would never have met him, but he was visiting one of the Reef islands at the very time I was there.'

'And what were *you* doing there?' Morgan asked, hearing this for the first time.

'Waitressing, if you must know,' Marcia flared. 'And you keep that to yourself. I've built up quite a reputation in this city. I had no past before I married into the Hartlands.'

'But the past is very real.' Morgan shook her raven head.

'I'm very good at putting things behind me, Morgan,' said Marcia bleakly.

Morgan looked away, blinking tears from her eyes. 'No one can deny that. I've come to you, Marcia, because you're the only mother I've got. I seem to be going through a period of distress.'

Instead of listening, Marcia gave an incredulous laugh. 'Really? And you one of the richest young women in the country!'

'I'd trade it all to be loved dearly. I have a brain, Marcia. Plenty of energy. I could make a good life for myself, like plenty of other people. The rich are a minority.'

Marcia laughed again. She came back and sat down, looking at Morgan with pity in her eyes. 'What would you know about struggle? About being a woman, young and on your own? I know what a miser E.J. was, but you always had his money behind you. You knew it was there, even if you couldn't touch it. You had an excellent education. More than I ever had. I had a pretty face. Men much prefer pretty women. It was the only bargaining power I had. You have millions!'

'Most of it is all tied up. I'm tied up, for that matter. To Ty.'

'And how is he now?' Marcia asked. 'Cecilia was the only one who was kind to me. Beautiful, golden Cecilia. She married Robert, you know, when your father loved her as well.'

'What?' Morgan's green eyes widened in shock.

'Clearly, darling, there's a lot you don't know. A tormented man, your father. He only married me as a way out. I couldn't complain. I married him for the same reason. It was a kind of pact. Everything went wrong with our lives.' Marcia's sigh was dredged up from the past. 'Believe what you will, Morgan, I was determined your life would be very different from mine. E.J. actually enjoyed taking you off me. The painfulness of it! But I was still too needy to go without the money. E.J. compelled me to get out.'

Morgan pressed a hand to her temple. 'But you just said you had money. Surely enough to take care of us both?'

Marcia flashed her a strange look. 'Your father changed his will. I didn't benefit at all. Neither did you.'

'But Cecilia said you did.'

'Cecilia was wrong.' Marcia smiled bitterly. 'The family believed what E.J. told them. I've never forgotten that reading. E.J. called me into his study, told me to sit down, unfolded the document and read it aloud without so much as a grain of pity. I got nothing.'

'But you could have contested it!' Morgan became excited. 'A wife is surely entitled to the largest part of her husband's estate.'

Marcia seemed intent on the magnificent diamond surrounded sapphire on her left hand. 'That's when E.J. introduced his scheme. After a short time, when you went away to boarding-school, I was to leave Jahandra. I didn't care. I always hated it. So big and so lonely, and that terrible man. The frightful, remorseless part was that I had to leave you. That was the bargain. E.J. got a grandchild. I got the money.'

'You mean, you sold me?' Even now all the old hurt flooded through her.

'I knew what it was like to be poor. It's bad enough on your own. It would have been impossible with a small child.'

'E.J. wasn't going to support me? His only grandchild?'

Marcia frowned, shifting in the yellow moiré sofa. 'He was quite prepared to break off his relationship with both of us. His terrible nature would not allow him to show it, but he was particularly interested in you. I had the feeling he had you picked out for Ty even then.'

'For Ty?' Morgan's distressed cry echoed around the elegant room. 'But that's crazy!'

'Is it?' Marcia's expression was tense. 'I'm quite sure E.J. knew what he was about.'

'Marcia!' Morgan stared at her in disbelief. 'I've gone all my life thinking of Ty as my enemy, my rival.'

'Have you?' Marcia bit her lip. 'The rivalry was encouraged. E.J. had to have his bit of fun.'

Morgan reached over and grasped her mother's hand. 'I am a Hartland, aren't I?'

'Of course you are!' Marcia declared explosively. 'Darling, would you release me, please? You're marking my hand. All that work around the station has made you terribly wiry.'

But Morgan was transfixed. 'Say it for me—as God is your witness, I am a Hartland.'

'Let go, Morgan.' Marcia's face looked deeply frightened.

'Say it!'

Marcia's silken cheeks were burning. 'Isn't this out of order? How could you be so disrespectful? What is it you're expecting to hear, some juicy scandal? Your father was some visiting musician?'

For a moment Morgan was sure she was about to faint. 'Why would you say that?' she whispered.

'Morgan!' Marcia could not ignore that pallor. 'What are you thinking about, darling?' she said in a rush. 'It was just something that came into my head. You've gone as white as a sheet. I'll get you a brandy.' She leapt up and went to an oval gilded table, pouring a measure of spirits into a crystal balloon. 'Here, darling, drink it. Why is all this so important to you? E.J. has kept his promise. You're rich. You can do anything you like. Go anywhere you like. Goodness, what more could you want?'

Morgan felt so strangely weakened, she swallowed most of the contents of the glass. It ran down her throat like liquid fire and instantly revived her.

'So you won't give me your word.' She handed Marcia the crystal glass.

'When it's not necessary, surely? This is madness, Morgan. Someone has put you up to it.'

'I've been listening to it all my life.' Morgan leaned forward, her beautiful hair clouding around her face.

'I'll try and find a photograph of my mother,' Marcia promised. 'She had just your slanted eyes.'

'What nationality was she?' Morgan demanded.

Marcia swung about angrily, the rope of pearls swinging around her neck. 'Irish, originally. That's where you get your temper. Plenty of the Irish have raven hair. You have to stop all this, Morgan. Thank God Philip wasn't here tonight. Imagine if you started all this in front of him. I can hardly bear to think about it.'

'He doesn't know you're a "scarlet woman".' Morgan gave a little broken spurt of laughter. 'Am I to take it, then, my father was a musician? Is that why I play so well?'

Marcia was obviously striving for composure. 'You're never satisfied, Morgan, unless you have a lot of drama. It's embarrassing, really. I suspect that dreadful girl— what's her name?—Camilla Ogilvie has been trying to upset you. Probably it makes her furious, the strong bond between you and Ty. She could even be out to challenge your inheritance. Have you thought of that?'

Morgan was trembling. 'No,' she said.

'You'd better believe it!' Marcia warned. 'There's always plenty of intrigue where there's money involved. Are you really going to play into her hands? *Am I a Hartland?* you ask. Of course you're a Hartland. Would E.J. have wanted you if you weren't? He would have tossed you out into the streets, with me. He was your grandfather, my dear. Have no fear of that.'

'And what of Ty?' Morgan could hardly force the words out.

'Darling, I know your torment.' Marcia looked down on her in her slender rose-pink suit, gold-belted, which revealed utterly beautiful dancer's legs. 'You're in love with him, aren't you?'

'The whole thing is crazy! I don't want to be in love with him. It's madness.'

Marcia shrugged. 'Love often is. I remember the first time I was in love. I thought I would die of it. Don't you think E.J. knew what he was doing, Morgan? He wanted you two to get married. You're an exceptional girl. You've proved it. E.J. put you through every test there is and you came out with flying colours. You're a fit person to take over where he left off. You're a fit mate for Ty.'

'For God's sake!' Morgan raged. 'Ty and E.J. fought continually. E.J. did insane things to wreck Ty's plans.'

'Except he was testing Ty,' Marcia insisted. 'You forget I know how E.J.'s mind worked. He wasn't just going to hand a pastoral empire to you. He had to make you both tough. Trial by fire, I think it's called.

'Except marriage has never crossed our minds.'

'Until now?'

'Ty is very practical.' Morgan's slender fingers began to twist. 'He goes straight after what he wants. A merger would solve a lot of problems. Not the least of it, it would keep the fortune intact. I don't think Ty would celebrate if I married someone who might threaten the Hartland empire. He has to take care of it. That's his job.'

A slight smile curved Marcia's lips. 'Allow for his feeling for you, Morgan. Ty always was someone who knew his own mind. Much as the two of you were compelled to fight when it came to anyone else, and that included E.J., he was always in your corner. Ty cares for you, Morgan. I'm quite sure of that. Since you've spent a little time and money on yourself, you're a striking young creature. Tonight you could have been lifted from the pages of *Vogue*. You have style. I know I could find you a score of eligible young men to choose from if you so desire. Philip will be so proud to see you looking exactly right. It's absolutely stupid we've been apart so long. Why don't you stay on with me for a time? I could introduce you to society. Properly dressed, you have the air of a little princess. Perhaps a little of the young Vivien Leigh.' Marcia broke off as a uniformed maid appeared in the doorway.

'Dinner will be served when you're ready, Lady Ainsley.'

Marcia stood up, her white chiffon dress falling away from her slim waist. She held out a hand to Morgan. 'Thank you, Heaton. We'll come now. I don't think you've met my daughter. Isn't she beautiful?'

Morgan almost laughed. Now, when it didn't matter, Marcia's maternal instinct had been reawakened.

CHAPTER SIX

MORGAN sat in her chair facing the solicitor, her small face impassive but in reality intent on everything he had to say. She wouldn't rest until she knew for herself if E.J.'s will could be broken. It wasn't the money, as Ty had believed, but the deeply rooted longing to have something entirely to herself. As things stood, she felt at the point of crisis. Her headlong physical reaction to Ty had shown her the extreme difficulties of the future. Men were men and they usually took what they wanted. She was really on her own, no matter how closely she had been drawn to the twins in the past month. Ty was their brother. Their adored brother. They would do whatever he wanted.

'I understand your feelings, of course, Miss Hartland,' the senior partner of the law firm was saying, 'but you must face the fact that your grandfather was a highly respected man, a legend in his own lifetime. Hartland Holdings were his to dispose of as he pleased. Most people would see it as a fair will. Although your grandfather did not give you the controlling interest, your status has been generously recognised. I'm bound to tell you it is highly unlikely that if you decided to contest this will, you would succeed. What you would succeed in doing is paying out a lot of money without the desired resolution. Regarding Jahandra homestead, you could reach a private settlement with your cousin. In that respect the will isn't carved in cement. It's unusual to have arranged it in this way. Perhaps observing you together, your grandfather formed the opinion you might at some point marry. It's the only view that makes sense. Have you not considered that might have been his purpose?'

'It certainly appears like that,' Morgan agreed quietly, 'but the thought of marriage had never entered our minds.'

The solicitor frowned. 'I'm sorry I can't tell you what you obviously want to hear. My advice is to accept your grandfather's wishes and get on with your life.'

Acceptance, a woman's theme-song.

That evening the three girls were invited to a big charity function—dinner and a parade of overseas fashions— and afterwards their party decided to go on to a nightclub.

'Count me out,' Morgan told Sandra as the girls repaired their make-up in the powder-room. 'Graham's attentions are getting a little too hard to handle.'

'I think it's more like you're feeling blue.' Sandra turned to stare at her. 'You want to go back to Jahandra, don't you?'

Morgan smiled. 'I keep repeating I'm a country girl. I've enjoyed myself immensely, Sandy. You know I have, but I seem to have so many things on my mind.'

'Ty promised he'd come for us,' Sandra said. 'I had a letter from him yesterday.' Sandra ran a comb through her shining curls.

'Oh, you didn't tell me.'

'You were out last night and this morning, and with all the preparations for this evening I forgot. Won't you come with us for a little while? We're all looking absolutely gorgeous. A pity to let it all go to waste.'

'I think I've had enough, thanks, Sandy. I'll never catch up with my sleep.'

'At your age!' Sandra scoffed, admiring their reflections in the mirrored wall. Sandra was wearing midnight-blue duchess satin with a deep heart-shaped neckline and long sleeves. Claire, talking happily at the opposite mirror, wore brilliant pink, and Morgan had allowed the twins to make her selection, a short, strapless evening dress in the shade that suited her best, emerald green.

'Legs like that need to be seen,' Sandra told her. That wasn't the only thing showing, Morgan thought. The faint swell of her breasts was provocative above the tightly fitting bodice with a row of tiny covered buttons running down one side. That single evening dress had cost more than she had formerly spent on herself in a year. She didn't own beautiful jewellery like the twins, so she had her long hair dressed in an updated chignon and wore a beautiful hand-made silk flower decorated with brilliants low behind one ear. The colour had been dyed to match her dress and satin shoes exactly, and she had been receiving compliments all evening. Especially from Graham. He was an attractive, articulate young man. Why couldn't she take to him? Morgan suddenly had a sinking feeling she was going to go through the rest of her life like this.

Graham insisted on driving her home, and, as he had picked the girls up, Morgan didn't have a great deal of choice.

'Aren't you going to invite me in?' he asked laughingly as Morgan walked up the steps to the foyer of the apartment block. 'I never get to see you alone.'

'Graham,' Morgan said, 'I'm going back home in a day or two. You've given us a wonderful time, but the worst thing that could happen is for you to become interested in me.'

He stroked her silky arm. 'Ah, but I have! What's the time? Gosh, it's early. You have no excuse not to invite me in for coffee. I always behave myself, Morgan. Well, most of the time!' His hazel eyes sparkled.

She took pity on him, shrugging. 'Coffee, then you must leave.'

'Absolutely!' he promised.

But being alone with her proved too exciting. In the lift he bent forward and kissed her cheek; his touch was very warm, solid, masculine. He was attractive, but not cataclysmic like a man she refused to think of. It was very quiet on the top floor, the décor a subtle deep pink and gold, and, as Morgan rummaged in her glittering evening purse for her key, Graham suddenly put his arms around her, almost groaning into her hair. 'Ah, Morgan, what the hell am I going to do about you?'

'I told you. Forget about me.' Morgan put her hands over his, trying to prise them apart.

'I want you to know you're the best thing that has happened to me! I never expected to fall in love. Actually, I have my life planned. Now you come along.'

'Passing ships, as they say. Please let me go, Graham.'

'It's not exactly crowded around here. Kiss me, Morgan. You're a real *femme fatale* and I'm a victim.' He turned her in his arms, his hazel eyes alight with desire and sudden determination.

'I don't think I'll offer you coffee, after all,' Morgan said smartly.

'Why don't you give a little?' Graham urged her, pulling her closer. 'You're so bright and beautiful, yet you're a mystery. You don't allow anyone to come close to you. I never have the slightest difficulty with other girls, yet you haven't displayed one reaction.'

'I suppose I could slap you,' she suggested.

'I'm hooked on you, Morgan,' Graham breathed, and lowered his head.

Of course Morgan ducked, and as she pulled away, her shoe hitting the door, he grabbed at her hands, kissing them madly.

'Please, sweetheart, I didn't mean to frighten you.'

'You're not frightening me, Graham, but I'm not enjoying it.'

'Please let me come in,' he begged.

'Regretfully, *no!*'

'So I'll kiss you out here,' he declared. 'A man has to show who's boss!'

The door behind them opened abruptly and a steely male voice sliced the air. 'I wouldn't if I were you.'

Ty loomed in the doorway, his lean, powerful body emanating male aggression, his blue eyes blazing.

'Ty!' Morgan exclaimed, trying to check the hectic flush that rose to her cheeks. 'Where did you spring from?'

His face remained hard. He didn't even look at her. 'And you're——?'

'Graham Ellis,' Graham supplied. So easily able to dominate in court, he was embarrassed and flustered. 'I take it you're Morgan's cousin. The twins speak about you often.'

'Say goodnight, Mr Ellis,' said Ty.

'Yes, I will.' Graham tried to sound casual but failed dismally. 'Goodnight, Morgan. Thank you for a very pleasant evening.'

It was almost painful to look at him. 'Goodnight, Graham.' She answered more sweetly than she would have. 'I enjoyed it.' And she had. Much of it. But she was back to resenting Ty's high-handedness. It was a powerful tradition.

Ty stood back while Morgan preceded him through the door. 'You have a definite knack for inciting a wide cross-section of males.'

'I suppose you might say that,' she returned coolly, though her blood was boiling. 'Couldn't you have warned us you were coming?'

'Warned you?' His tone was edgy. 'This penthouse belongs to me.'

'Sometimes *I* feel the same way.' Morgan threw her evening bag down on a side-table. 'Was it really necessary to play the heavy with poor Graham?'

He gave her a derisive smile. 'Personally, I think I moved at the right minute.'

'You weren't listening, surely?'

'I wouldn't have missed a word. Hooked on you, is he?'

'How despicable!' Morgan fumed.

'Perhaps. I can see through all your little masks. You were starting to panic, but nothing in this world would make you admit it, or the fact you're pleased to see me.' Ty moved lithely back towards the nest of sofas.

'And you're still the same. I could have moved Graham on.'

'He looked like a determined man to me. Let me have a look at you.'

She threw back her head. 'Are you kidding? I was ten times safer with Graham.'

'Do me a favour and turn around. That's one heck of a dress.'

'Considering how little there is of it, it was a frightful price.'

'Turn around, Morgan. Don't be shy.'

'Me, shy?' she said disdainfully, and twirled towards him.

Ty's shapely mouth curved in mockery. 'I know just how he felt.'

'That's the definition of a woman, is it? To please and attract men? I'm looking for other alternatives.'

'I know that, and I understand what you're saying but, Morgan, you were subverted. You were reared as a boy with a man's goals. You won't let yourself be happy as a woman.'

'Oh, please suggest the ways!' She felt as though his eyes were consuming her. She drew a ragged breath into her lungs and pulled the flower from her hair, throwing it down on top of her evening bag. Her head was aching from the unaccustomed champagne and the pins of her hair were suddenly insufferable.

'I'm not complaining right now,' he said drily, watching her long dark hair uncoil around her face and down her back. 'What kind of a reception is this? You haven't even asked how I am.'

'I only have to look at you,' she said, deliberately gazing away.

'Then why don't you? You're prowling around like a little cat.'

'Oh, God,' she said in an odd voice. His face was full of shadow and light. 'What time did you arrive?'

'Reception told me I'd only just missed you. Who the devil was that?'

'You mean Graham?'

'The oversized schoolboy.'

'Actually he's a big-time lawyer.' A sense of excitement was making her tremble. Morgan sat down, slipped off her satin shoes and tucked her legs under her. 'See all the flowers around the room? He sent them. Every day. He hasn't missed from when we met.'

He looked at her, amused. 'Then why were you finding him such a drag?'

Morgan sighed. 'God knows. How's Cecilia?'

'Very well. She sends her love. She really wants you to come home. She can't wait for you two to get going on all that redecorating.'

'I have lots of ideas myself.' For the first time, Morgan smiled. 'You have no idea of the beautiful things we've seen. The twins have taken me everywhere. I have a splendid new wardrobe.'

Ty leaned back, the light glinting on his dark gold hair. 'Do show me.'

'I'm sorry. I don't have complete confidence in either of us.' Some note in his voice made her shiver. 'Have you had anything to eat? Can I get you something?'

'Yes, please.' He looked at her as she sat, noting the long, gleaming black hair, lustrous, slanting eyes, the sheen of gold on her olive skin; her back was straight, bodice clinging to her small, uplifted breasts, the emerald green skirt flaring around her so that she looked as fragile as a doll. She was anything but relaxed. Under the familiar challenge she was burning with nervousness. 'Morgan?' He saw her tremble.

'I won't have this, Ty.'

A slight smile curved his mouth. 'A month is a long, long time.'

'I happen to know you've been all over the place, tying up loose ends.'

He frowned in agreement. 'Believe it or not, E.J. left a lot of things in one hell of a mess. We were so used to the brilliance of his heyday, we overlooked the fact he was getting old. I've had to double-check everything. Then there was that insane spree designed to create difficulties for me. He dumped a small fortune.'

'Sounds as if he could have been of unsound mind,' she suggested darkly.

'You ought to check who you talk to. E.J. always prided himself on his devious mind.'

'I'm not with you,' she protested, seized by panic.

'Try McEwan and Chandler.'

Morgan took a deep breath and her head went up. 'You mean the solicitor I spoke to took it into his head to inform you?'

He raised an eyebrow slightly. 'Nothing so unethical. Nevertheless, I heard. Solicitors talk to each other.'

'I'm shocked.'

'The way of the world, Morgan. Not a damn thing's safe.'

'So tell me, are we poor?'

'Would you care?' He looked at her steadily.

'Yes,' she suddenly admitted. 'It's amazing how easy it is to get used to spending money. Are there problems, Ty? I demand to know.'

'Sure, there are problems,' he acknowledged. 'There are problems in any business.'

'I want to share them.'

'Of course you do, but not tonight. I feel like re-
laxing. When things settle down I want to take you
around all our holdings. Everything we own. I don't
think you're fully aware of the extent of E.J.'s interests.
I didn't even know he owned thirty per cent of Nyruna.
He seems to have kept so much to himself. He was always
a very secretive man, but now I'm discovering things are
a great deal more complicated than we first thought.
Even Henry is dumbfounded, and he was E.J.'s lawyer
for years. It's going to take time to get a clear picture.
There's a whole complicated world of real-estate devel-
opment as well, though one of the companies is ailing
badly.'

Morgan raised one delicate eyebrow. 'So it's even more
challenging?'

His eyes travelled over her. 'Nothing and no one in
this world is more challenging than you.'

Morgan moved abruptly. The very last thing she could
do was let loose the wildness that prowled between them.
'Can't I get you a drink?' she began. Movement was the
key.

'Any Scotch in the place?'

'Definitely. Claire has an admirer, Bryan Wyndam—
you know him. He's very partial to the malts of Islay.'

'The twins are well?' he asked casually, his expression
another thing.

'Of course. We've had a marvellous time.'

'And where are they tonight?'

Morgan walked quickly into the kitchen for some
crushed ice. 'Gone on to a nightclub,' she called. 'It's
really not my scene.'

When she returned to the living-room Ty was slumped
deeper into the couch. She passed him the glass and he
took it with one hand, pulling her down beside him with
the other. 'Relax,' he encouraged her, 'Morgan, the cat.'

The breath caught in her throat. She shook her head and he lifted a hand and ran it around her nape. 'I'll always take the greatest care of you, Morgan. I promise.'

'Care? Would you call it that?'

'Running away won't solve our problems.' He tipped the glass towards his mouth and drank. 'Whatever happens, I won't lose total control.'

'You've got power, Ty. Don't use it.'

'Power?' he questioned. 'I'm a fortunate man. It doesn't mean all that much to me.'

She laughed, like a splintering of glass.

'That dress of yours.' He regarded her. 'I don't think it comes up far enough.'

She looked down, ignoring the swell of her breasts. 'I assure you it's the height of fashion.'

'It's the kind of dress to cause a raging storm. I want a painting of you. Who's a fashionable portrait painter these days? Rupert Cranston?'

She stared at him. 'And how would you suggest I pose, like a witch?'

'I have to admit you look terribly like one.'

'Except, of course, I'm not wicked.' She looked around her helplessly. She had to move before her emotions mastered her.

'No, stay.' His arm shot out and encircled her narrow waist, pulling her inexorably towards him so that she was forced to come to rest against his shoulder. He tossed off the contents of his glass and set it down on the long, glass-topped coffee-table.

'I went to see Marcia,' she told him, as though it were terribly important.

'And?' This time he drew her across his body so that he could look down into her face.

'There's a lot I didn't know.' She couldn't help herself. She let her eyes move hungrily over the fine bones of his face: chiselled cheekbones, cleanly defined mouth, firm yet sensual, the little sun lines fanned out from his brilliantly blue eyes. He hadn't shaved since early morning, but the faint shadow of his beard only emphasised his virility. She had to question herself deeply. Why was she allowing herself to lie in his arms, staring up into his eyes? What frightened her so much was her uncontrollable fascination.

'Well?' he prompted gently, a sensual quality to his voice.

'Did you know my father was in love with Cecilia?'

'That's old news, Morgan.'

'No one told *me*.'

'Sorry. From all accounts, everyone was in love with my mother. It happens like that sometimes. Certain women are given dangerous gifts.'

'Men, too.' Morgan stared up at him, desire searing her.

'What else did she tell you? Or rather, what did she continue to keep hidden?'

Morgan's eyes flickered. 'Hidden? She said she rushed headlong into marriage with my father. A rebound situation, for both of them. Obviously it didn't work out. I'm afraid I upset her. I asked her who exactly in the family I was like.'

His sleek eyebrow shot up. 'A tricky one.'

'What's tricky about it?' she wanted to know.

'How long did she take to ponder?' His blue eyes, so intense, became hooded.

'I'm like my grandmother. Marcia's mother.'

'She has means of demonstrating this, of course?'

Morgan frowned, her green eyes bewildered. 'Suddenly there's mystery in the air. I've gone all my life thinking one thing, now I'm being forced to consider another.'

'All that's happened, Morgan, is you must see things as we do.'

'Who's we?' Her head came up.

'No one you need worry about.' He stared into her eyes. 'There's my mother. And me.'

'And you think you're on to something?'

'It depends entirely on what you want, Morgan.'

She fell back again, against his arm. 'Well, I handled that badly, didn't I?'

'Tell me what you mean.'

'You're out to prove I'm not E.J.'s granddaughter?'

'I thought you were the one trying to prove that.'

'Oh, my God!'

'Don't run off the rails,' he warned her, bluntly.

She gave a little wild laugh. 'Why is everyone suddenly interested in the past? No one was before. No one ever questioned my rightful place. Until now. Camilla Ogilvie talks to me. *"How strange you are!"* I've suddenly grown two heads.'

He groaned. 'Whatever you are, it's fine with me.'

'You're an arch manipulator, you know that?'

'Uh huh.' He looked down into her eyes. 'Little did we know when you grew up we'd have all these problems.'

'We wouldn't have had a problem at all, if you hadn't kissed me,' she said immediately.

'You lie!'

'I do not! We were doing OK. A few fights.'

'A few hundred,' he contradicted her.

'I really don't remember.'

'No wonder, there were so many of them. Then I kissed you.'

'That took care of everything,' she said.

'Absolutely. Maybe it was the drama of the day, or I'd been waiting very patiently.'

'I'd like to find out why,' she suddenly said passionately. 'And that brings us back to E.J.'s will. Are you sure he never told you?'

'Now, then,' Ty said crisply, 'are you doubting my word?'

'Did he tell you anything?'

'Of course.'

'I knew it!' Morgan pushed back her head and stared up at the ceiling. 'All that privileged information, and I never heard a word.'

'What he told me was I was totally overlooked. Even Henry didn't know he had made an about-face. I never suspected, Morgan, he had arranged things as he did.'

'So you decided to make love to me?' she suggested, green eyes outraged.

'And you couldn't have been more co-operative.'

'Oh, you demon!'

'Call me Lucifer,' he mocked.

She pushed up, hovering helplessly, as he pinned her. 'You deliberately covered every angle.'

'I'd like to. Of you!'

'Why, you devious...'

'Go on. Excite yourself.'

She whirled on his lap, meeting his vivid blue eyes. 'You are the very last man in the world I would give myself to. *Ever!*'

'You're already mine,' he said with deceptive lightness.

'And if I am I'll never face it!' She was nearly crying with rage.

'Of course you will. No one can say I'm not patient. We'll take it very slowly.' One hand came up to encircle her throat. 'Keep still, Morgan. I don't want to bruise you.'

'I think you'd enjoy it!' She gritted her small teeth.

'No. There's absolutely nothing I would do to hurt you.'

'Except hypnotise me when it bloody suits you,' she accused him.

'Language!' he tutted. His blue eyes burned into her. 'You are so beautiful.'

Their faces were barely inches apart. She could feel his warm breath on her cheek. She loved him so much,

she wanted to weep and weep. Instead she drew a little
shuddery breath, then leaned forward to touch his mouth
with her own. She realised it was dangerous, but it was
something she couldn't control. Everything about them
was so highly charged.

Ty kept very still and Morgan pressed her mouth on
his. She put up her hands and rested them on his
shoulders. She'd never thought she would do such a
thing. Yet she had. But her subconscious had only allowed her to pursue her hidden yearnings in half-
remembered dreams. He might have been a statue he sat
so still, but his mouth was warm and so desperately exciting. She wanted to trace the clean raised outline with
the tip of her tongue, but she had scarcely begun before
he turned her back violently over his arm, dominating
her with his body and crushing her mouth in a hot wave
of male desire.

The same force that impelled her now controlled him.
He was holding her, kissing her with an exultant triumph,
driving her head back so that he could explore her mouth
more deeply. She was pinned by his lean body. He had
placed it precisely for his enjoyment. Passion was a wild-
fire, writhing and curling and leaping, gaining ground
by the moment. She wanted him to crush her like this.
It was unbearably exciting.

The tiny bodice of her evening dress had moved down,
almost exposing the nipples of her breasts. The gleaming
emerald material seemed to be stretched tighter as her
flesh swelled in sexual arousal. The thought of his
touching her made her whole body shake. If this was
what it felt like to be a woman, it was terrifying, like a
free fall from a mountaintop.

His mouth ran down her throat and the curve of her
body. He lifted her, expertly finding the side zipper,
though it was totally hidden, and moving the lightly
boned bodice down around her waist. Now, even as his
hands moved to capture her breasts, she cried out, mag-

netised yet aghast at the searing thrill that lanced through her.

Her body, her breasts, were so highly sensitised, the lightest brush of his hands was exquisite pain. If he set his mouth to her nipples... She arched back instinctively, her small cries unrestrained but he only proceeded to lift her higher in his arms so that he could take her in the way that totally subjugated her.

Her nails raked his sleeve, the paisley velvet of the sofa. Anything. If he had not been holding her so tightly, her whole body would have thrashed.

'Morgan.' His voice was tight, tense, matching the ruthlessness of his expression.

'Please,' she gasped wildly. 'I can't stand this.'

'I want you.' His blue eyes devoured her, her face, her throat, her delicate torso. His hand drove down her heart-shaped body, moving over her silken legs, and she gyrated madly.

'No, Ty, *no*! I won't let you.' Her whole body was flaming, shockingly alive in every nerve, every cell.

His hands moved over her legs, over and over again, as though he was seeking to control the remorseless urge to know her body.

'Oh, please, Ty, no more,' she begged. 'What do you want me to say? I love you.'

'This is hell!' His eyes were furious, blazing.

'I can't believe what we're doing.' She pressed her half-naked body to him, pleading for reassurance.

'I hadn't planned it this way, but it *will* happen. Every time we're together. I want to take hold of you every time I lay eyes on you. I'm shocked at what I feel. Do you really think you're the only one? I *will* have you, Morgan. You know it. It's inevitable.'

'Do you have to take everything?' she asked wildly. 'Can't you do something when you see this coming?'

'What would you suggest?' he asked violently. 'Seduce a total stranger? I want no other woman, but you. I didn't want it. It happened.'

'I must get dressed,' she told him in an agonised voice.

'No, don't. Let me look at you.' His voice startled her with its tenderness.

'The twins will be home.'

'That's all that's saving us,' he said with wry humour. 'Besides, Lagoon Maidens don't need clothes. I told you. All you need is a gold earring and a coronet of flowers.'

'Don't talk to me like this, Ty,' she whispered. 'I can't bear it.'

'You're not making it easy for me either, cuddling into me like that.' His voice was tender but harsh.

'I'm sorry.' She fought for control, pulling the emerald sheaf around her, her fingers nerveless. Finally Ty had to draw up the zip.

'How did you find it, anyway?' she asked shakily.

'I was looking at you every minute. Are you going to fix your hair?'

'Does it need fixing?' She looked at him with huge eyes.

His hand came up, moved a long gleaming lock off her naked shoulder. 'You're filled with anxiety, aren't you?'

'Why is it like this, Ty?' she begged. 'Sometimes I think I would let you do anything to me. Anything. Just shocking!'

'You're so innocent.'

'I know, and it's awful. I never knew anything about this world of erotica.'

'I wouldn't expect you to.'

'Of course. Naturally. Experience is for men.'

'You want experience?' he asked drily.

'Who would want it? It's terrifying.'

'Goddam right! Real passion is a mystery, and it doesn't reveal itself to everybody. You're young, I understand your panic.'

'I don't think you do. It's so physical.'

'You want it, don't you?'

She sighed very deeply. 'I want it so much, I'm in pain.'

The weeks before her twenty-first birthday passed in a flash. Looking back, Morgan recognised they were the happiest of her life. She had never lived a normal life under E.J. She could see that now. Underneath her station uniform of sturdy shirt, moleskins and riding-boots was a deeply creative person fighting to get out.

They all had a marvellous time doing up the home-stead. The project was so big, and time was so limited, they called in the design house of Paxton & Partners to advise and help them. In his youth Ian Paxton had been a well-known dealer in decorative objects and fur-nishings, but helping friends successfully decorate their houses opened up a whole new line of business. As the designer himself observed, there was no shortage of 'things' about the homestead. What was needed was a lighter, cosier, more contemporary look. Morgan and Cecilia had a few other stipulations, and as the weeks went by the homestead underwent tremendous change.

They seemed to spend their days surrounded by swatches of fabric and colour-charts. Everything was painted, repapered, re-upholstered, except for the mar-vellous Chinese wallpaper in a large sitting-room. They decided to turn it into a garden-room because it gave directly on to the wide back terrace. A small army of workmen lived and worked on the premises while the restoration and refurbishing was going on. Furniture was moved around, the best pieces retained for the major rooms, the rest relocated or stored away. Superb new curtaining opened up new vistas of the garden and brought in light, and a magnificent Indo-Herat rug that had languished for years in a store-room was given professional treatment and put down in the entrance hall where it flourished and repeated the deep blues in the huge stained-glass window over the first landing and the melon of the new velvet on an ornately carved Indian sofa.

Morgan found a dozen horse paintings stacked away behind traditional large landscapes, and she carried them down in triumph to decorate the study.

'I want your opinion.' She grabbed Ty one afternoon as he called into the house for a few minutes.

'If it's anything about colours, forget it!'

'No, it isn't. It's the most marvellous surprise!' She was nearly dancing with joy. Ty shared her passion for horses, and three of the paintings, in particular, were captivating.

Because Ty worked every night in the study, its re-decorating was being left to last, but Morgan had arranged the paintings along one wall: spirited renderings and traditional stances of magnificent subjects, arabs, thoroughbreds, from silver through a rich chestnut to gleaming black.

'What do you say, Mr Hartland?' She waved her hand like a magician.

He moved right into the room and walked across to the paintings to inspect them. 'I couldn't ask for anything better,' he said finally, his expression one of surprise and enjoyment. 'This one here, the Andalusian showing its paces, is the pick of them. The arab is good. So's the Appaloosa. Where did you get them from?'

'One of the store-rooms.' She came to stand at his shoulder. 'Aren't they just beautiful? I love paintings of animals, especially horses. What about that big painting Gary Knox did of you playing polo? I love that. It would look great here. We'll get Steven to send it over.'

He turned to look down at her, vibrant and full of life. 'You're having a lot of fun, aren't you, elf?'

She nodded. 'It's frantic trying to get it all finished in time, but yes, I'm enjoying it immensely.'

'You must be seeing yourself in another light as well.'

'Meaning?' She looked away from the Andalusian and up at him.

'You're a very creative person. The twins tell me they just nod their heads. Clearly my mother is impressed.'

'Doesn't everyone love decorating?' she asked in amazement.

'Some people have no talent for it at all.'

'Ah, well, we have Ian. He's so knowledgeable and *funny*! I would have to live a hundred years to catch up with him. It's going to cost an awful lot of money, I'm afraid.'

'This is where we live,' he said carelessly. 'Besides, the last time anyone tried their hand at it was well over eighty years ago. I have a meeting in Grantley tomorrow. Want to come with me?'

'Of course.' She lifted her raven head. 'I strongly recommend keeping an eye on you.'

In fact, they saw little of one another. The transformation of the house occupied all Morgan's time, and Ty was making his position as head of Hartland Holdings official by calling on the other stations in the chain and making surprise visits to the headquarters of their various ventures. It was a period of consolidation and the weeks flew by.

It was during the final stages of the redecoration that Ian Paxton flew out one of the principles of his firm, a statuesque redhead by the name of Sarah Stacey, who fell so madly in love with Ty, it was dreadful to see.

At least for Morgan. For the first time in her life she knew what it was to experience the pangs of jealousy. And Sarah was nice: warm, friendly, expressive. The sort of woman who gave out to others. Which meant

Morgan's pangs of jealousy were worsened by acute self-disgust. Basically Ian had brought Sarah out to show her what had been done. It was a major project and they were all very proud of it, but Sarah, being the creative artist she was, had her own input. She decided on a new chintz for the garden-room just in time and brought a fresh approach to the treatment of the master bedroom. It was Sarah who spied some very old Chinese wallpaper panels tucked away in a cabinet and had them framed and placed in Morgan's bedroom, which she had re-painted the soft green of the leaves in the beautiful tree peony panels. Famille rose pinks, touches of blue and green was the theme, and Morgan's bedroom suite emerged rather more beautiful than it would have been.

To her credit, Morgan offered congratulations. Sarah had served a long apprenticeship in design, and despite her inherent excellent taste Morgan was without so many skills.

'Experience, dear,' Sarah told her kindly. 'You have considerable ability, you know. Why don't you think of a career in interior design? With your money, you could start your own business. Bring in the best people, and five years on I would say you'd be a name to reckon with. You're only scratching the surface of your skills.'

'I'd never thought of it, Sarah,' Morgan said soberly.

'My dear, you have to do something. It would be asking too much of a talented young woman like yourself to be satisfied with just sitting around.'

Morgan smiled wryly. 'There's plenty to be done on the station.'

Sarah opened wide her lovely blue eyes. 'Heavens, why would a beautiful young woman want to play jackeroo? There are any number of young men looking for work. Why would you take it off them? I can't bear to think about it. Take your piano playing, for instance. You're very, very good. I was amazed when you first started to play. I thought maybe Ty had exaggerated. He's so fond

of you, but he wasn't exaggerating at all. You're a fine
pianist. You could have hurt your hands in the crazy
situations that seem to have taken place in recent times.
Your grandfather must have been an unusual man. To
this day my father takes my hand when we cross a busy
road, and that's on the pedestrian crossing. Yet the
stories I've heard about you are really scary.'

'Nothing happened to me, Sarah.'

'Unusual family.' Sarah held up some silk in a brilliant peacock blue. 'How's this for the scatter cushions
in the main guest-room? We need something bold.'

'Perfect,' Morgan agreed.

'This really is a marvellous place.' Sarah stretched and
looked around her.

'You should have seen it before we started.'

'Gloomy, I agree. Ian did take photographs, but one
could see exactly how it could look. It's an enormous
advantage if the family has a host of possessions to
choose from. How extraordinary to grow up amidst all
these splendours. I had such an ordinary childhood,
hence my thirst for beauty. Ian and I agree the main
reception-rooms are the most beautiful we've ever done.
I'm glad you and your aunt didn't decide to undertake
it all on your own. Professional advice. That's the real
key to success,' Sarah declared confidently. 'This is just
the sort of place Ty deserves. Such a *stunning* man! So
charming, yet so forceful. The mixture is just right. I
must say he makes all the men of my acquaintance seem
slack.'

'You're divorced, aren't you, Sarah?' Morgan deli-
cately enquired.

'Yes, dear.' Sarah looked up from one of Ian's water-
colour sketches to give her a smile. 'My dear husband
was a compulsive gambler. I just couldn't take it. I simply
upped and moved off. No child to think of, which saved
a lot of suffering. I want children, of course, and I have
to hurry. I'll be thirty-four next birthday.'

'You look marvellous,' Morgan told her sincerely. 'Would you want to continue to work?'

'That would depend entirely on my husband,' Sarah smiled. 'I must say the lucky woman who marries Ty would have everything she wanted. Long periods in the country. Longer periods in the city. A varied life-style. One could take to the limit.'

'Not with Ty. He wouldn't go for it.'

'Nonsense!'

'He wouldn't, Sarah. This is Ty's life. I think I should warn you.'

'Whatever do you mean, dear?' Sarah stared at her.

'You're very attracted to him, aren't you?'

'Oh, my God, does it show?'

'It isn't unusual.'

'I should think not. He must be the catch of the century.'

'A lot of women have expended a lot of energy trying to catch him.'

'Thanks for telling me. You're a good girl. And what about you? Tell me to mind my own business if you like, but what are you going to do when Ty marries?'

'Half of this place is mine,' Morgan pointed out with wry humour.

'Yes, I know, dear.' Sarah clicked her tongue sympathetically. 'Your grandfather made it difficult for you. I can feel you love the place.'

'I love the station more. Everyone would wish for all this beauty and comfort, but it's the land that gives Jahandra life.'

'It doesn't frighten you?' Sarah asked with genuine attention.

'In what way?'

Sarah shook back her rich fall of hair. 'It's so huge, it's humbling. I keep thinking of the numbers of people who get lost out there.'

'One has to obey the rules, Sarah. The rules are there for our own protection.'

'I'm sure.' Sarah gave a little shiver. 'Yet your aunt and the girls have an enviable life-style. They're so beautiful, so sparkling. They know everyone. They go everywhere. When do they do that?'

'Whenever they like. That's OK. Ty doesn't mind. He wants them to be happy.'

'His wife could do that, surely?' Sarah persisted. 'Isn't a wife's place by her husband's side?'

'Well, it was in traditional marriages.'

'Ty is a traditional man. Accept it. I'd hate you to think he was the sort of man who would say nothing if his wife took off at a moment's notice. Ty would want the woman he loved around all the time. Count on it. He would want the mother of his children to rear them in the traditional way. He's no chauvinist, but he's no push-over, either. Any woman who wished to marry Ty would have to consider seriously what her life-style would be. Ty's view of a wife is his closest companion. Not someone else's companion. He's a very dominant man and his life-style only serves to entrench his masculinity.'

Sarah blinked black furry lashes. 'Are you trying to warn me off, Morgan?' she asked.

'What do *you* think?'

'I think you're a little witch.' Sarah laughed. 'How did you come by those great slanting eyes?'

'My maternal grandmother.'

'Ah, yes, Lady Ainsley. I've seen her a few times at functions. She's even more attractive than her photographs. How come you don't live with her, or near her?' Sarah asked.

'My grandfather reared me,' Morgan replied lightly. 'Jahandra is my home.'

'Then you have a problem, haven't you, dear?' Sarah looked at her directly. 'Forgive me, but it must have come to mind. I should think Ty would marry fairly soon. His wife wouldn't care to share their home, much less you. As Ty is the head of all your family interests, I suppose the solution would be for you to settle elsewhere.'

'Maybe I don't want to settle elsewhere,' Morgan said spiritedly.

'But you couldn't stay here.' Sarah looked bewildered. 'You sound alarmed.'

'Well, dear,' Sarah picked up a piece of cardinal red damask and studied it carefully, 'no offence intended, as they say, but you must see there could only be one lady of the house.'

'And I'm supposed to step aside?'

'You, with not a care in the world!' Sarah smiled. 'As I hear it, Morgan, you're a very rich woman. Your knight in shining armour could turn up right out of the blue. He would carry you off as soon as possible. You'd have a wonderful home all of your own.'

'No one is attempting to kick Ty out, I notice,' Morgan said bluntly.

'Would you really want to do that?' Sarah opened her eyes wide, a habit that was fast becoming familiar.

'I haven't yet learned total self-sacrifice. Everyone makes the immediate assumption I am the one who has to go. Personally, I don't understand why. Ty and his bride can build something just as big up the road. After all, my grandfather left him more money than he left me. I say let Ty take off!'

It was said with such fire, it gave Sarah considerable food for thought. She was without her usual sparkle for the rest of the afternoon.

CHAPTER SEVEN

IT WAS Cecilia who decided to give a smallish dinner party to celebrate the near completion of the house. Work would continue over many months, but the main rooms would be done in time for Morgan's gala twenty-first.

'We'll ask Steven and Sue. The Masseys. I think we'll have to ask the Ogilvies or we'll never hear the end of it. What about Jessie Stannard and her two boys? We need some young men. How many is that?'

'Fifteen,' Sandra answered promptly. 'Let's settle for twenty. What about Pat O'Donough, Morgan?'

'What about him?'

'May he come?'

'Pass.'

'I don't mind Pat,' Claire said. 'He has a couple of things going for him. He's a big handsome male. He'll inherit Parkhurst.'

'Which all adds up to a big fat nothing so far as I'm concerned.'

'We won't ask him if you don't want him, Morgan,' said Cecilia soothingly.

'No, that's all right,' Morgan shrugged. 'I'll practise my feminine wiles on him while Sarah continues her courtship of Ty.'

Sandra giggled. 'She's so *obvious*!' she whispered. 'I could have sworn her hair was smoking last night.'

'She does seem to have it rather badly,' Cecilia was forced to concede. 'Still, she's a charming woman, don't you think?'

Morgan sprang up from her seat. 'A real profession-al. I feel I have to get moving. Anyone want to go for a ride?'

'As long as you don't do that insane galloping,' Sandra agreed. 'Count Pat in, Mamma. Wait until he sees the new Morgan. He's going to flip.'

As a prediction it was spot on. They were determined to keep it small, and the dinner party numbered twenty. Their guests were delighted to have an advance preview of the house, all except Camilla, who was enraged at the sight of Sarah, wearing a long glittering black sheaf that made the most of her tall, voluptuous figure leading the party around, holding affectionately on to Ty's arm.

'Struth!' Pat shook his flaming, leonine head. 'Camilla took years to make that progress. What gives with the decorator? Is she making a play for Ty?'

'Who knows, she may succeed,' said Morgan crytically.

'Poor old Camilla looks on the point of mental col-lapse,' observed Pat.

'So does her mother. I'm not twenty-one yet, but I've learnt that absolutely nothing is certain in this life except leaving it. I swear no one but Ty has been allowed to enter Camilla's mind. Her mother must have started the indoctrination in the cradle. I feel sorry for her tonight.'

'So do I,' intoned Pat. 'Is that dress glued on?'

Morgan looked towards Sarah. 'She has a wonderful figure!'

'She sure has,' agreed Pat enthusiastically. 'She's not in the first flush of youth, though.'

'Youthful enough. Early thirties. I tried to tell her, but she thinks the mistress of Jahandra can somehow be away most of the time.'

'Is it that serious?' asked Pat.

'Oh, yes, I promise you.'

Pat tightened his grip on her arm. 'Ty looks better than ever, lucky devil. He just keeps collecting beautiful women.'

'That he does!'

Camilla waited her moment and then drew Morgan aside into the folds of the curtains. Her expression was so formidable, she looked more than ever like her mother. 'Who does that woman think she is?' she demanded.

'You mean Sarah?' Morgan looked over to where Ty and Sarah were standing. Sarah was talking with great animation. Ian, her mentor, was standing back, selflessly giving her her head while she described how to handle pattern on pattern.

'The woman is an opportunist,' Camilla snorted.

'I like her.'

'Of course you would. You take to anyone I don't fancy. How ever did she get so friendly with Ty?'

'He encouraged her,' Morgan said simply.

'Oh, my God!'

'It's obvious they're having a good time,' Morgan pointed out with a sideways glance. 'If I were you, Camilla, I'd forget Ty. You're spoiling your life.'

But Camilla was heedless. 'You haven't changed a bit, have you?' she said almost bitterly. 'Under the new chic is Ty's little imp of a cousin.'

'All right,' Morgan shrugged. 'You won't let me help you. If you're not happy you can always leave.'

'I'm here at Cecilia's invitation.' Camilla gave her a haughty stare.

'With my forbearance,' Morgan said patiently. 'I know you think I'm trying to get at you, but I'm not an unkind person. I mention it because I can't bear to see one of my own sex get hurt. Ty doesn't love you, Camilla. You can't change that. There's not enough time in the world for it. Why don't you concentrate on Mark Stannárd? He finds you attractive.'

'Oh, you're clever, aren't you?' Camilla flushed. 'It will be the day when I take advice from you.'

'I can easily cross you off my birthday list,' Morgan said tartly.

'You *wouldn't*!' Camilla looked shocked.

'Well...I suppose the invitations have gone out. Sarah and Ian are staying for the gala.'

'They're *what*?' Camilla's cheeks were the clear red of her dress.

'We thought it would please Ty.'

'Oh, you little bitch!'

Morgan gave a little twirl to escape. Camilla wouldn't accept the truth, not even if they got the Pope to present it.

Yet the dinner party turned out a great success. Their guests were not returning home until the following day, so there was no reason to call a halt.

'One would think it always looked like this!' Sue Tyson announced, looking around the magnificent dining-room which was enormously enlivened by recoloration, splendid new drapes and a reshuffling of paintings and ornaments.

'How nice of you to say so.' Sarah flashed a brilliant look towards her host. 'That's what one aims for, of course. The woman Ty marries will inherit a marvellous house.'

'She'll have me for a start,' Morgan added mischievously.

'I don't believe a word of it!' Sarah laughed promptly. 'I'm convinced you'll be married before you're twenty-two.'

'Hear, hear!' Pat lifted his wineglass, his smile besotted. 'Just one trip to Sydney and she's come back a raving beauty.'

'Sweet of you to say so.' Morgan returned the gesture.

'What do you think, Ty?' Pat looked towards the head of the gleaming table. 'What do you think of your little madcap cousin now?'

Ty looked at her with his intensely blue eyes. 'I never doubted for a moment she could look like this. In fact, I've never had a complaint at any time.'

Sarah's glowing head swung back sharply at his tone. The indulgence in his handsome face was on open display. But then she could have sworn something more significant was determinedly concealed. Astonishment set in.

It was well after two before the household finally retired, already agreeing to meet for a late brunch. Morgan hung her dinner dress up: a short plum silk brocade, very simple, with a wide toning waistband to show off her tiny waist. The fabric was beautiful and it suited her colouring, lending plum lights to the raven sheen of her hair and contrasting with her skin and her emerald eyes. Towards the end of the evening Pat had become very excited, flushed of face and faintly slurred of voice, asking her how long it was going to be before she agreed to marry him. No matter what she said, he persisted with it as though her objections were to be expected but of no real consequence. It was obvious he was taking it as a preliminary game. How smug was the male! Yet no blinder than a female. If looks could kill, Sarah would have been neatly laid out.

Morgan was on the point of climbing into bed when she thought to check if there was sufficient wall lamps left on in the corridors. Switches weren't all that easy to find in strange houses. Someone might wish to get up during the night. She opened her door and peered out. Trust Cecilia to think of it. She was just about to withdraw when she saw Sarah emerge from her bedroom wearing a remarkable blue satin and lace peignoir over a matching nightgown. Morgan caught the gleam of lipstick, so obviously she wasn't yet ready for bed. Sarah

didn't even look her way. She swept away in the direction
of the double stairway, her hair glowing deepest crimson.

Interesting! For complex reasons Morgan decided to
follow her. She had the sinking feeling Sarah was going
in search of Ty, and she was proved to be right. Life
was full of the most fearful shocks. She crept along the
corridor, then peered over the banister, looking down
towards the wide entrance hall. The triple archway
blocked a lot of her view, but she heard Sarah's nicely
judged exclamation of surprise.

'Oh, Ty! I thought everyone was in bed.'

Liar! Morgan collapsed back. Ty had the eyes of an
eagle hawk.

'Can I help you, Sarah?' Morgan heard him ask.

'Aspirin. I find I have a slight head.'

It wasn't original, but it was a start. They moved off
and Morgan flew down the stairs, saved in the nick of
time by an eight-panelled coromandel screen. She slipped
behind it as they moved back into the hallway.

'I didn't realise there would be some in the bathroom,'
Sarah said. 'I rarely open a medicine chest.' A slight
pause. 'I thought everything went off terribly well
tonight.'

'It did.' Ty's voice was sexy and smooth. 'Thank you
for your contribution.'

'Any time.' Sarah's voice too was low and husky. 'This
is really my kind of house.'

'We'll be more than happy to give you the highest
recommendation.'

Quite rightly, Morgan fumed.

'You're awful, Ty. Cruel. You know how much I'm
attracted to you.'

'No. I had no idea.'

Morgan could just see his mocking smile.

'All right.' Sarah gave a guilty little laugh. 'You know
I came down in the hope of seeing you.'

'You're a very attractive woman, Sarah,' he told her, in Morgan's opinion egging her on.

Oh, you bastard! she thought wrathfully. How frightful that her vision was limited. She could only see through the crack between panels.

'And determined,' Sarah confirmed. 'You'd better be prepared for that.'

'I won't hold it against you.'

Sarah gave a little excited moan. 'At least won't you kiss me for my trouble?'

'Certainly.'

Just like that! No hesitation.

Morgan didn't understand how he did it, but he turned Sarah so that even her voluptuous figure was completely obscured by his superior height and the width of his shoulders.

Oh, you fiend! It was hard for Morgan not to dash out from behind the screen and proclaim his infamy to the heavens. She would like to tip the screen on him, but it was very heavy.

'Goodnight, Ty,' Sarah said in a voice so subdued that she must have been kissed senseless.

'Goodnight, Sarah. Pleasant dreams.'

I'll bet! Morgan was sure Sarah had the Arabian Nights in mind.

She fell back against the wall, waiting for the soft pad of Sarah's footsteps to subside. Obviously Sarah didn't fall into bed on a first date. Take your time and make sure of it.

'When are you going to decide to come out?' Ty's voice asked acidly.

'When I know your girlfriend's gone,' Morgan called angrily.

Ty walked across to the screen, got one hand behind it and yanked her out. 'I know you had woeful training, but this takes the cake.'

'I had nothing better to do,' she said fierily.

'My poor little Morgan, you're jealous!'

'I'll survive. You're a real skunk.'

'Come on,' he jeered. 'The party's not over. Sarah is a very attractive and worldly woman.'

'So how come you're not joining her later?'

'Sometimes I don't understand myself. I was certainly invited.'

'I know. I was behind the screen all the time.' Her great green eyes flared.

'Did you think I didn't recognise the feet? Who else has child's feet? Who else would hide behind a screen to check on my behaviour?'

'I'm like you. I trust no one,' Morgan said arrogantly, flashing daggers.

'So why do you look as if you're about to cry?'

'That's not sorrow, Ty, that's disgust!'

'You get very disgusted about nothing,' he said testily.

'Do you men know anything about monogamy?'

'So who's married?'

'And when you do, move out. I was here before you.'

'Don't flash malevolence at me, you little imp.' He scooped her up bodily and bore her back into the drawing-room. 'Do you think you could try to curb your imagination, or at any rate, keep your voice down? It's as clear as a bell.'

'You think the rules are different for men?' she demanded, flinging her hair back.

'This is a party. At parties one is supposed to have a lot of fun.'

'I'll show you fun!'

'No, I'll show you,' he ground out. 'It's the only way I can keep you quiet.'

And that was the way Camilla found them, Ty kissing Morgan savagely, while her slender arms flailed away at his tautly muscled back. So intent were they on one another, Camilla had to rush at them with blazing, hate-filled eyes.

'Oh, I knew it! I've always known it!'

Ty lifted his dark golden head, his inner turbulence equalled by a hard exasperation.

'What the hell are you on about, Camilla? And what are you doing down here? Don't you women ever go to bed, or do you prefer swanning around in next to nothing?'

Camilla stared at him with the greatest intensity. 'And now we know who *you* prefer,' she cried venomously, throwing off all pretence of playing the guest.

'You saw yourself as a contender?' he drawled arrogantly, lifting his head in a characteristic high-mettled gesture.

Camilla ignored him. 'All that antagonism!' she moaned. 'It only concealed this!'

'And what's this?' Morgan demanded, nearly incandescent with rage. 'How dare you rush around my house taking all and sundry to task? It's quite disgusting. I told you your mad passion was all on one side.'

'Ty and I had reached an understanding,' Camilla blazed.

'Twaddle!' Morgan was burning with frustration. 'Utter balderdash. Ty has a whole cupboard full of women. One of them was just down here in a nightgown that would leave yours for dead. Diaphanous, I tell you. I could see the freckles on her.'

'I'm not worried about that decorator person,' Camilla flashed, 'so spare me your little tricks. Ty has never held me like he was just holding you.'

'Where are your wits? You're too tall, that's why. He thinks he can throw me around like a doll.'

Ty gave a maddened laugh. 'This is like something out of an American soap. I'm down here quietly turning out lights, and I'm attacked by no less than three women wearing minimal clothing. If I've learnt anything, it's try and steer clear of them.'

'Lots of luck!' Morgan quipped, drawing her robe around her so that nothing was revealed. 'I'd appreciate it, Camilla, if you'd go back upstairs rather than attempt to scream the place down. I have a nice little karate chop and I'd be delighted to use it. You all seem to think I'm some kind of an idiot, happy to take your bad manners and your abuse. The reason Ty was kissing me was to shut me up.'

'I've found it's the best way,' Ty supplied.

'This man is a rotter,' Camilla cried.

'You're absolutely right. Burn all his love letters.'

'What love letters?' Ty asked sardonically. 'Listen, does anyone mind if I lock up? Do you girls know what time it is?'

'Gosh!' Morgan looked at the face of the gilt mantel clock, surprised. 'I didn't know it was that.'

'There are always one or two stragglers,' Ty told her grimly.

'For God's sake!' Camilla slumped down in a Louis chair. 'Are you trying to tell me, Ty, we're through?'

'You'd better believe it!'

'How did you ever get yourself into this crisis situation?' Morgan asked more kindly. 'Get mixed up with Ty and be prepared to pay for it.'

'Go, upstairs, Morgan,' Ty suddenly clipped out in a hard-driven voice.

She flashed him a brilliant look. 'We'd better start dividing the house up into zones.' Nevertheless the expression on his face shook her. 'You'd better come with me, Camilla. You can't sit there all night.'

'Correct again,' Ty added shortly.

'I always knew it in my heart,' Camilla wailed. 'I'll get even with you, Morgan, if it's the last thing I do.'

Camilla was not present at brunch served in the beautiful new garden-room. Her parents evidently had not been told of the abrupt demise of their plans, because they both ate heartily, sharing in the general conversation. Sarah, in a mulberry silk shirt and matching linen slacks, pulled up a chair beside Ty and slid into it with a little comment that set everyone laughing. She looked the very picture of health, beautifully groomed and clear-eyed, her glowing hair bouncing with life. Morgan on the other hand felt as if she was teetering on the brink of a precipice. Underneath the glossy surface the atmosphere was simmering with passion and intrigue. Ty had brought Camilla to her feet, promising her instant retribution for any pain she attempted to inflict on Morgan, but Morgan felt in her bones Camilla would take her jealousy as far as she could. Camilla had an ego that would never end.

By one o'clock, apart from Ian and Sarah, they were down to their last guest. Pat was determined to make the most of his heaven-sent opportunity to get close to Morgan, and he suggested they go for a ride and take a swim in the creek if they felt like it.

'Wear you little red bikini,' he suggested, very happily.

'Play the gentleman,' Ty advised, 'or you're in deep trouble.'

'He's a pretty complex character, Ty,' Pat observed after Ty had gone down the stairs on his way to the jeep. 'What does he mean, I'll be in deep trouble?'

'Oh, I think you will know well enough.' Morgan stared after Ty's lean, powerful figure. 'Sometimes he comes in handy.'

'I never know for sure what he's thinking,' Pat frowned.

'All right, what goes on here?' a voice called gaily from the door. 'Oh, there's Ty!' Sarah lifted a hand to shade her sun-dazzled eyes. 'I wanted to have a word with him.'

'Race away,' urged Morgan drily.

'I will.' Sarah flashed them a dazzling smile. 'I really could get used to this station life.'

Morgan and Pat watched as Sarah ran after Ty, catching him up just as he switched on the ignition. A short exchange followed, then Ty leaned across to open the passenger door and Sarah hopped in.

'Atta girl!' Pat jeered beneath his breath. 'She's beginning to act like one of the family.'

'Maybe she figures she might be.'

'You're joking!' Pat looked at Morgan in amazement.

'I admire ambition in a woman, don't you?'

'Camilla was certainly acting strangely. I just know someone put her nose out of joint.'

'Some people can't take good advice,' Morgan pointed out. 'It's hot. We will go for a swim.'

Patrick had lived all his life with horses and he was the ideal companion for a hard gallop. They tore across the daisy-strewn flats, Pat taking up the challenge to be first at a station landmark, a huge desert oak that stood alone at the top of a sharp rise. Pat was a tireless rider, but Morgan was better mounted. Sultan flew with his characteristic long strides, but suddenly out of nowhere a doe carrying a joey in her pouch rose up from behind a tall mound of flowers. Her hide was the same reddish brown as the earth, affording her the best possible camouflage.

Morgan pulled on the reins at once, but the highly strung Sultan propped violently, unseating Morgan's slight body, and she was thrown sideways. She saw it all coming, so she gathered herself to roll. This wasn't her first fall and it wouldn't be her last. The thick carpet of flowers would break her fall, but as chance would have it a fallen log carried there by storm water lay half hidden by a clump of spinifex grass. She crashed into it, bruising but not seriously hurting herself, but a snake had chosen the decaying log for its retreat. Disturbed, it struck, lightning-quick, and Morgan, half dazed, looked down at its large, light brown body before it slithered away angrily.

'Morgan!' Pat shouted, dismounting rapidly and running towards her.

'Snake!' she gasped. 'Don't move me.'

'Where did it get you?' Pat looked around wildly.

'The arm!'

On the near horizon, marked by the desert oak, Pat looked up and like a miracle saw the jeep. He stood up and waved his hat frantically in the universal cry for help. Sultan now stood over Morgan in an attitude that could only be discribed as protective, lowering his head while she lay spread-eagled on the thick carpet of wild flowers. Her beautiful skin appeared pallid, almost waxy, and her eyes were opening and shutting as though overcome by sleep.

'That's Ty!' Pat shouted. 'Keep perfectly still, Morgan.' He was starting to panic. He would much rather the snake have bitten him. He could see the swelling on Morgan's arm. It was already turning purple.

He was trying to fashion a bandage from the tail of his shirt when Ty brought the jeep to a screaming halt.

'Morgan!' He took in the situation at once. 'What the hell are you waiting for, Pat? You know what to do.' He ripped the torn section of the shirt out of Pat's nerveless hands and fashioned it very deftly into a bandage. 'Morgan,' he said harshly, 'do *not* go to sleep.'

'I feel sick.'

'I know you do, but keep your eyes open.' Ty applied the bandage above the wound, issuing orders to Pat at the same time. 'There's a knife in the glove-box. Matches. Get them and bring them to me.'

Pat raced away, grateful Ty was taking charge. Seeing Morgan lying there so helpless affected him dreadfully. His brain wouldn't work, whereas Ty was swift and methodical.

Ty made tiny cuts at each fang mark, then lowered his head, sucking the wound by mouth and pausing to spit out the venom. When he was satisfied, he gently removed the bandana from Morgan's neck and tied it snugly above the first bandage. Morgan was still conscious, but she looked very pale and clammy.

'I'll get you back to the house,' Ty told her, slipping his arms beneath her slight, prone body. 'Follow us up, Pat, with the horses. I recognise those puncture bites. We have the serum. That's it, Morgan,' he encouraged her. 'Keep your arm down low. I'll have you home in no time.'

Even though Ty's quick action had arrested the spread of the venom, they had to stop while Morgan retched her heart out. Ty held her head, talking calmly to her all the while, telling her she was over the worst of it, cradling her in his arms until she was ready to go on.

At the homestead Cecilia was galvanised into action, rushing ahead to locate the correct serum. She stood at Ty's side while he administered it, her face anxious. Afterwards, with the wound washed and dressed, Ty carried Morgan to bed, where she fell into a sick sleep. She had lived all her life in the bush, even in a region where one could step over a snake every day, yet she had never been so unlucky as to fall on top of one. It was the worst sickness of her life, she considered. She was still nauseous, but her stomach was bone dry.

When she awoke at intervals, Ty was still there, though it was Cecilia who stepped over to the bed to ask how she was.

'Terrible!' Morgan whispered each time. 'I've never had a snake do that before.'

In the early hours of the morning she awakened suddenly, staring directly into Ty's eyes. He was sitting in a chair beside the bed, looking as though he hadn't had a wink of sleep.

'How's it now?'

'Wonderful,' she told him. 'My stomach seems to have settled. I'd better not move.'

He put out his hand and smoothed her hair off her forehead. 'How many lives is that now you've drawn on?'

'I'm not sure, but you've saved at least four. How's Pat?'

'Shocked out of his mind. The last time I saw him he was sitting up in bed crying.'

'Poor old Pat!' Morgan slanted him a faint smile. 'Do you think I'll pull through?'

'Len will be here in the morning to check you over, but yes, I think you'll be fine.'

'I want you to know I'm grateful. I only went with Pat because you took off with Sarah.'

'I have a feeling Sarah might want to leave the day after tomorrow.'

'I know. I'm sorry.'

'No, you're not.'

'Anyway, I learned a lot.'

'And what was that?'

'Go easy on the vinegar and more on the honey.'

He smiled. 'Isn't that what I've been trying to tell you all the time?'

'I'm going back to sleep now.' Her long eyelashes began to droop.

'I'll be here.'

'Thank you.'

She put out her hand and he held on to it.

The week before Morgan's party the presents started to arrive. Soon an entire room was stacked with boxes of all sizes.

'We'll display them in the billiard-room,' Aunt Cecilia decided. 'People do like to see their gifts on show.'

'Then we'd better start on it tonight,' Sandra suggested. 'It's amazing how much is there.'

'I truly never expected it!' Morgan exclaimed as she stood in the double doorway, staring in. 'I'm overwhelmed by everyone's thoughtfulness.'

'What a pity Sarah had to leave,' Sandra said slyly. 'You know something I don't?'

'I think she thought there was a possibility of snaffling Ty.'

'Well, it was a great idea but it didn't work.' Sandra began to pull the wrapping-paper off a large box. 'Helen and John Philips,' she read. 'Oh, look, it's a ... what?'

'A sculpture.'

'Something for the coffee-table?'

In contrast with the stark white modern sculpture, a silver fruit-basket followed, crystal galore, porcelain, dinner services, linen on a lavish scale. There was a beautiful biscuit figure of cupid from Patrick, a magnificent Wedgwood jasper-ware vase from his parents, six beautiful Waterford decanters and a number of very pretty clocks. After a half-hour they started to get rather tired. 'I'll go and get Claire to help us, lazy creature,' Sandra announced, struggling up from the rug. 'She can fold the wrapping-paper if nothing else. There's a mountain of it. I say, doesn't it look great? You seem to have an army of figurines. And birds. The big porcelain peacock is my choice. I'm sure it's modelled after something by Kandler. It would look marvellous against a screen. Would you like coffee to keep us going?'

'Love it.' Morgan looked up from admiring a silver rose bowl. 'It looks as if we might be here half the night.'

There was nothing to indicate who had sent one small flat package. From the feel of it, Morgan was sure it was a small painting or possibly a decorative frame. She had already unwrapped an art nouveau silver frame. The paper was rather odd, not at all in keeping with the occasion. Most of the paper had been specifically designed for a twenty-first birthday. The very severity of the paper on this package sparked her interest. She held it in her hands, holding it up to the light, then she slowly un-wrapped it.

A striking male face looked back at her. She would have recognised it anywhere. It was a framed glossy photograph, obviously a publicity photograph, showing a man dressed for the concert platform, black jacket, white tie, holding a violin in the crook of his arm.

She didn't move. She sat as though she had been frozen over.

She knew then that somebody hated her.

'My God, just look at all this stuff!' Ty, on his way from the study, put his head around the door. 'Now I know what they feel like at royal weddings. Most of this will have to be stored away.'

Morgan was in deep shock. The pain was spreading from the region of her heart out to her limbs. She had the feeling nothing would ever come right again.

'Morgan?' Ty walked over to her, alerted by her utter stillness, then the tightly shuttered expression on her face. 'What is it? Are you ill?' He crouched down beside her, taking the photograph out of her hands. 'Good God!' he said, in a deeply shocked voice.

'What a way to learn,' she whispered desolately.

'Learn what?' His tone was angry, fiercely protective.

'Please, Ty.' She turned to him with tortured eyes. 'That's my father!'

'More like a cruel joke.'

'Don't.' Her head fell forward. 'You know it. I know it. Now we both understand.'

'Understand what?' he asked harshly.

'I'm nothing. Nobody.'

He put his arms around her and lifted her from the floor. 'We don't know who he is, Morgan.'

'He's my father,' she insisted, starting to shiver. 'And I'm his imbecile daughter. I'm not family, Ty. I never was.'

'Let me take you upstairs.'

'I'll give you back everything. Everything. It's all yours.'

The twins walking casually back into the room, stopping in astonishment as they saw their brother comforting Morgan.

'What's wrong, Ty? Is she sick?' Sandra asked anxiously, hurrying forward. 'Maybe she never got over the snake-bite.'

'Possibly,' Ty clipped off. 'Sandy, do you think you could go upstairs and turn the bed down? Claire, tell Mother I need her.'

'Of course, Ty,' the twins replied as one.

No sooner had they left the room than Ty swooped on the photograph, shoving it behind the skirt of a long trestle ingeniously covered in gold-fringed green velvet to dress it up.

'Never.' Morgan shook her head. 'You can't hide it, Ty. Not now. I feel changed forever. An heiress to nothing.'

Cecilia came rushing into the room in answer to the summons, her lovely face dismayed. 'Whatever has happened, Ty? She's been so well.'

'You know who I am, Cecilia?' Morgan asked, lifting her head. 'I'm no one.'

'Whatever is she talking about?' Cecilia looked with alarm to her son.

'Someone sent her a photograph. I've shoved it behind the table. I don't want the girls to know.'

'A photograph?' Cecilia frowned. 'What sort of a photograph?'

'It's my father,' Morgan said very quietly, and fainted.

The twins accepted that Morgan felt a little sick and they quietly returned to the task of unwrapping the presents. 'She fights everything so hard,' Sandra exclaimed. 'She should have stayed in bed longer, instead of getting up.'

'This is the way I want it, Morgan,' Ty told Morgan after the girls had returned downstairs. 'Nothing has changed. You've been a Hartland all these long years.'

'Who did this?' Cecilia demanded. 'Who would be so cruel? And in this way?'

'You believe it, don't you, Cecilia?' Morgan asked. 'You haven't seen the photograph, yet you know.'

'I know, Morgan, you're one of us,' Cecilia told her firmly. 'Marcia is your mother and you were reared as a Hartland. The same thing.'

'Not the same thing at all. You knew about Marcia. The life she had led. You knew she was pregnant when she married?'

Cecilia pushed her hand through her copious blonde hair. For once it was disordered. 'Please don't talk, my dear. You look so pale.'

'Let her talk,' Ty ordered. 'Let her get the poison out of her system.'

'She denied it, you know. I asked her.' Morgan lay back, her black hair fanning out over the lace-edged white pillows. 'She swore E.J. was my grandfather. I believed her. I believed her because I wanted to belong. I belonged for twenty-one years. Now I don't.'

'Nonsense!' Ty spoke in his normal authoritative fashion. His blue eyes sparkled, very direct and hypnotic. 'None of this matters to us. We've already discussed this, Morgan. Time after time.'

'How awful!' She stared from one to the other. 'You knew all the time?'

'None of us exactly knew, Morgan,' Cecilia told her quietly. 'We had our private thoughts.'

'Then how did you allow it to happen? Why was I reared a Hartland?'

Cecilia considered. 'E.J. loved you in his way. He certainly meant you to have your inheritance.'

'I'm not entitled to it.' Morgan's eyes filled with tears. 'I'm taking so much from you and nobody was going to say a word. Not you. Not Ty.'

'Why would we?' Ty sat down on the side of the bed, taking her hands firmly between his own. 'E.J. wanted a grandchild. He got you. I expect he knew all about Marcia. Maybe he didn't. Either way, I don't think he cared.'

'But I'm his image. I'm that man's image.'

'Is she?' Cecilia looked worriedly at her son, who sat staring at Morgan's pale, traumatised face.

'The same eyes, brows, mouth. The resemblance can be seen at a glance.'

Morgan gave a broken laugh. 'He was a musician, you know. A concert violinist.'

'What?' Cecilia drew back, her expression startled.

'It must have been a publicity photo.' Morgan shifted restlessly in the bed. 'He must have visited the Reef. Nearly all our overseas visitors want to fly there. It's so beautiful, so tropical, so romantic. I think Marcia would have been very pretty.'

'Lovely!' Cecilia sighed deeply, her gaze introverted. 'We need time, Morgan, to work this thing out. We need to know who sent this photograph.'

'Not Marcia,' Ty said briefly. 'I think I recognise the malicious hand.' He gave a faint smile. Like a tiger.

'Who, darling?' Cecilia wanted to know. 'We must find some way to force them to admit it. This whole thing has to be kept quiet. Morgan is a Hartland. A Hartland she remains.'

'I shall try to find my father.'

Cecilia hesitated, but only for a moment. She reached out to Morgan. 'Of course, we don't know. We're making enormous assumptions purely on the basis of a physical resemblance, but I'm almost certain the man you speak of, the concert violinist, was killed in a plane crash on a return flight to America. There was a great deal of publicity at the time. It was a disaster. I believe he was an American citizen, but of Russian origin. I even remember his name.'

'Go on.' Morgan looked at her, mesmerised.

'Zakarov. Mikhail Zakarov. The only reason I remember is because I'm greatly interested in music, as you know. The violin is my favourite instrument. I had absolutely no idea this young man who was only at the beginning of a brilliant career had spent any time on the islands. Why do you mention it?'

'Because Marcia forgot herself. She handed me a clue. She said, "What is it you're expecting to hear? Your father was a visiting musician?" She met him on the islands, not the man she later married. Or maybe they were both there, Marcia deciding who was the greater catch. She never expected to become pregnant. That's Marcia. She acts first and thinks later. It must have come as quite a shock to know she was carrying me.'

'Do you really think it wise for her to talk?' Cecilia asked Ty worriedly. 'She's as white as a sheet.'

'It's not every day one finds out they're illegitimate.' Morgan laughed a plaintive sound.

'And who gives a damn, since you never knew any different? You're a Hartland,' Ty told her deliberately.

She turned her head to stare into his eyes. 'I'll give it all back to you. As soon as I can. I can't think of anything now.'

'You'll rally, Morgan. You've got plenty of guts.'

'Have I?' she asked faintly. 'I feel as if I'm falling apart.'

'So do I.' Cecilia collapsed into a chair. 'On the eve of her birthday. This is quite unreal.'

'She had to find out,' Ty offered sombrely.

'I'm Miss Zakarov. Is that exotic enough for you?' Morgan laughed. 'Morgan Zakarov. I knew I looked like a girl in my ballet book. "You're like my mother," Marcia said. I intend to take Marcia apart.'

'Good.' Ty approved the first flicker of fire in her eyes. 'Marcia should be introduced to the truth. But once you know it, Morgan, you'll have to file it away. We don't intend to hand the Press any spicy stories. I'm sure you won't want to hurt Marcia, either.'

'Why not? She hurt me.'

'The world regards you as Edward Hartland's heiress,' Ty said decisively. 'That's the way you've lived all your life. If Zakarov really was your father and he was involved in that tragic incident, it serves no good purpose to reopen old wounds.'

'It's wrong for me to take what is not mine. I have no claim at all,' Morgan said with finality.

CHAPTER EIGHT

MARCIA was amazed to see her, her expression faltering when she saw the depth of animosity in Morgan's eyes.

'Why, darling, where did you spring from?' she cried expressively, trying as usual to ignore reality. 'Sydney is the last place I expected to see you at the moment. Is something wrong?'

'Try betrayal,' Morgan shot back. 'As soon as Ty turned his back, I stowed away on the freight plane. An awful trip.' She pushed past Marcia and walked into the house. 'You have to be one of the great unsung actresses of all time!'

Marcia was wearing a dress of softest green, and now it was echoed by the pallor of her face. 'Go into the drawing-room, Morgan. Don't yell at me out here.'

'Who's yelling?' Morgan asked. 'You mean you're terrified someone might hear me speak?'

'That, and you're obviously angry about something.'

'Angry?' Morgan tapped her breast. 'Angry, dear God!'

'Really, Morgan! Go in. Sit down.'

'You think you can handle me like you've handled me before? No way, Mother, the day of reckoning is at hand.'

'Rubbish!' Marcia exhaled dramatically. 'Whatever it is, Morgan, we can sort it out.'

'Let's see,' Morgan looked down at her watch, 'it's nearly four. What time will Philip be home?'

'Please leave Philip out of this,' Marcia said.

'It will sure make things uncomfortable for you if I won't. I have to admire the way you do it, Marcia.

Practice, I expect. I have something in my bag I want you to see.'

Marcia gestured firmly with her hand. 'The drawing-room please, Morgan. Please don't drop any of your bombshells here.'

'*My* bombshells?' Morgan laughed. 'We're going to talk about *your* exploits, Mother.' Morgan walked into her mother's white and gold drawing-room and deposited her carryall on the floor.

'Whatever in the world is all this about?' Marcia followed her, standing her ground coolly.

'Your mistake was in thinking I would never find out.' Morgan delved into the bag and withdrew a large yellow envelope.

Instantly Marcia sat down, staring in fascination at the glossy photograph Morgan drew out.

'Do you know this man, Mother? Do you know anything at all about him?'

Marcia drew back fastidiously. 'Should I?' she asked in apparent bewilderment.

'Look again. Shall I find your glasses?'

'I don't *wear* glasses.'

'Even if you did, you wouldn't need them. Who is he, Mother? I think you owe it to me to speak the truth.'

Marcia leapt up, shocked. 'I don't know what you're talking about. You're such an odd girl. So intense. You hate and resent me for leaving you the way I had to.'

'I don't hate you, Mother,' Morgan said. 'I hope to God I don't hate anybody. What we're talking about is disillusionment. So deep I can hardly speak of it.'

'I know better than that,' Marcia said. 'You hate me. E.J. turned you against me. Where did you get that photograph, anyway? Did he leave it for you?'

Morgan shook her head. 'Someone sent this to me as a birthday present. How's that for hating? I'm simply not in that class.'

Marcia looked at her astounded. 'You mean someone sent this through the mail?'

'No other way.'

'But for what purpose? That man is a complete stranger to me.'

'I'm the image of him,' Morgan replied.'

'I don't see it.'

'You can't even bear to look at the photograph.'

'What are you trying to do, ruin me?' Marcia suddenly clutched a chair, as though afraid of fainting.

'Who is he, Mother?' Morgan asked bleakly.

'Who the hell do you think he is?' Marcia suddenly exploded.

'My father.'

'How can he be? You're a Hartland. You've just been left a fortune. Are you going to pass that up?'

'Yes, I am.'

'I won't allow it, you little fool!' Marcia's voice shot up in panic and outrage. 'Do you really think after all these years I'm going to allow you...'

'It's already too late, Mother. Ty knows. So does Cecilia. They have always known, I suppose.'

Marcia's silken cheeks had lost all colour. 'You mean, you showed them?'

'Face it, Mother. I'm not a Hartland. I never was.'

'Oh, yes, you are. We earned it. E.J. wanted a grandchild. He got one.'

'Did he know?' Morgan said wearily.

'Unlike you, I told him nothing. E.J. was a visionary. He saw things in the future. He never had any time for women, but he recognised the spunk in you. He saw the bond between you and Ty. I believe he started to plan then. His empire had to remain intact. The man who ran it had to have the right woman. She had to be specially trained for the job just as royalty train their own. The responsibilities, the demands of a certain way of life, are understood and accepted. I believe E.J. reared you to inherit the Hartland chain, but as Ty's wife. I never expected anything else. That was his plan. Understand, all that really mattered to him was the survival of his empire, not people. As his heirs, you and Ty excelled. That's all there is to it.'

'So you believe I'm entitled to my inheritance, even though I'm not a Hartland?' Morgan asked ironically.

Marcia's lovely face hardened. 'Understand me, Morgan. You are a Hartland. What did Ty and Cecilia have to say?'

'Would you believe it, they're with you?'

'Because they're worldly wise.'

'Did you love him, Mother?' Morgan asked finally.

'Of course I loved him,' Marcia said in a strangled voice. 'I was crazy for him. You could say possessed. He belonged to another world, an exciting, glamorous world. He had his music. I had nothing. No family to speak of. No money. All I had was my looks. I had to use them. Grasp life where I found it. I've never forgotten.'

'How could you?' Morgan retorted. 'I'm the image of him.'

'That you are.' Tears suddenly rolled from Marcia's beautiful eyes. 'I was so young. So lonely. You've no idea what it was like. You have to fall passionately in love to realise how obsessed one becomes. I was helpless to resist. So was he.'

'And he was killed?'

Marcia bent her head. 'We had such a short time together. I wanted to die, too. It took a lot of courage to keep going. He was going to send for me.'

'Perhaps,' Morgan said quietly, her gaze fixed. 'Could you not have told me? Could you not have found that special time to tell me about my father?'

'Morgan, I've just explained. You're a Hartland. E.J.'s heiress,' Marcia insisted, dominated by a powerful self-interest which included her daughter.

'I'm going to give it all back, Mother.' Morgan looked back at her in rebuke.

'You don't know what you're talking about,' Marcia cried, weeping now.

'Oh, yes, I do. Unlike you, Mother, I cannot continue to live a lie.'

It took an extra day for Ty to track her down. When Morgan returned to her hotel room in the late afternoon, Ty rose from an armchair to greet her. Although the grimness of his attitude threatened her, she met him, as usual, head on. 'What I like about you, Ty, is you bypass all the rules.'

His brief laugh was anything but apologetic. 'Wouldn't it have been easier for everybody if you'd simply told me what you intended to do?'

'Not as I see it,' Morgan said briskly, setting down her parcels. 'Tell me, what's the difference between you and everybody else?'

'Hotel managers usually recognise me.' He gazed at her, arrogance all over his handsome face.

'I'm sure that doesn't give them the authority to allow you into my room.'

'I certainly wasn't going to wait in the foyer,' Ty replied abruptly. 'After all these years, can't you turn to me when you're in trouble? It took us hours to realise you'd fled.'

Morgan scooped up a silk cushion from an armchair and threw it on to the bed. 'I had to talk to my mother alone.'

'So tell me,' Ty demanded, getting a firm hold on her hand and dragging her down into the chair.

'Why not? I grew up with orders. At first she denied she had the answer to the great question.'

'Well, she would,' Ty nodded curtly. 'So far nothing had induced her to speak.'

'Right. Then she got angry. The point is, she made a bargain. Marcia is a lot tougher that I thought. The fact I'm not a Hartland has nothing to do with my inheritance, it seems.'

'E.J. certainly saw it that way.' His blue eyes skimmed her brittle elegance.

'Do you really think he knew?' Morgan's voice was muffled.

'Probably not at the beginning,' Ty considered. 'But then it no longer mattered. It's all true?'

'Yes. Aren't you happy? My mother and E.J. between them made me live a lie.'

'It's not going to be helpful if you overplay the dramatics. You don't have to look on it that way. E.J. accepted you as his grandchild. If he hadn't wanted you, you would have left with your mother. Surely you realise that? To all intents and purposes he adopted you.'

'And my mother allowed him to.' Her green eyes flashed.

'Marcia obviously believed she was doing something positive for you.'

'How terrifying. As though the promise of wealth is a substitute for mother love.'

'Wasn't that how she explained it? Life hadn't been easy for her. She lost the man she loved. She lost the man she pressed into marriage. She wasn't going to lose out a third time, and she determined in her own way it wasn't going to happen to you.'

'Let's say she's an opportunist, and let it go at that.'

'So what are you going to do now? You'd better tell me.'

She lifted her head and tilted her chin. 'Bow out with your blessing.'

Ty's firm mouth hardened. 'I think you had better start looking at this from everyone else's position. To the rest of the world you're a Hartland. I understand at this time you're all for the grand gesture. You just want to pitch the money at me and get it all over with.'

'I certainly do,' she said fiercely.

'My foolish little firebrand! Don't you think you should check again with E.J.'s will? Whatever his private thoughts, and he was no fool, he regarded you as his granddaughter. Someone special. He couldn't tell you. He didn't know how to. But by his lights he loved you. You may not feel this, but you were the only person on earth he praised. He didn't do it to your face. He didn't intend to spoil you, but he was proud of expanding your spirit. What matters is you were the granddaughter he wanted. Would you agree with that?'

'No, I wouldn't,' Morgan said obstinately, eyes brilliant. 'E.J. didn't want a granddaughter. He wanted a male heir.'

'You're wrong,' Ty pointed out laconically. 'He wanted a pair. Two people he had specially trained. He recognised in you his own great love of the land. It speaks to you as it spoke to him. E.J. was more terrified of the wrong woman than you can ever imagine. He had the experience with his stepmother and his own wife. Marcia might have been plucked from a hothouse, so badly did she fit in. All the time he must have been thinking what would happen to his empire after he was gone. Its very survival depended upon being administered by the right people.'

'Well, naturally you were the right person,' Morgan mocked him, in a turmoil of love and the old hostility. Yet his positive, forceful presence strengthened her.

'There was no one else,' Ty explained. 'He was haunted by the old feud, but in the end he chose to ignore it. Maybe I was descended from the stepbrother who had caused him so much pain, but I understood power. He knew I could handle it when it was given to me!'

'So who's arguing?' Morgan swept up. 'It's all waiting for you, Ty the Great.'

'I'd hoped it was waiting for us,' he said shortly.

'You know that's impossible now.' She looked out of the huge picture window at the blue, glowing harbour. 'In my mind I have no legal or moral right to the Hartland fortune.'

'Of course not. You're so high-minded, it hurts. But do you have a moral commitment to unmask your mother? To cause a scandal?'

Angrily she turned on him. 'Are you asking me to continue living a lie?'

'For twenty-one years you believed yourself to be a Hartland,' was his cool response.

'So?' She shook back her heavy, silken hair.

'E.J. adopted you without signing a few papers.'

She laughed. 'Obviously he had to have someone.'

'That's it, then! He had you.' Ty stood up, towering over her. 'You were a beautiful child and very, very bright. He reared you for a purpose.'

'For you?' She stared up into his wonderful eyes.

'That's the primitive part. He was a power-broker. We have to recognise that. It seems obvious now that E.J. intended us to marry. He deliberately encouraged our rivalry. Both of us would rather die than be cut off from our heritage.'

'Except it's not my heritage at all. No, stay away.' She threw up her hands. 'I don't want you to touch me.'

'That's your wounded heart talking,' Ty said quietly, standing very still, 'not your head. Jahandra has been your home all your life. There's no reason why you should ever leave it. There were strings attached to your inheritance, you know. You have to marry me.'

Colour flooded her cheeks. He could see how volatile she was. 'How arrogant, how high-handed you men are! We're almost at the dawn of the twenty-first century, and little has changed.'

'Marriages of convenience will always be acceptable,' Ty pointed out, almost casually.

'Except I couldn't tolerate such a situation. My life has been miserable enough. I have the brains and the ability to go it alone.'

His eyebrows rose. 'Would I want you if you didn't? And make no mistake, Morgan, I do want you. You'll make a good partner. I'm not in the market for a hostess.'

She felt so angry, she was frightened of losing control. 'You're saying this could be a b-b-business arrangement?' She was almost stuttering.

'Shameless of me, I know. I shouldn't be at all surprised, however, if the sexual urge takes us. I've only made love to you a few times, and I don't think you could call your response tentative.'

'So I curse myself!' she shouted. 'You don't love me.'

'You're woven into the fabric of my life,' he admitted.

'I don't love you, either,' she flashed, feeling the terrible sense of loss right through her bones.

'That's a plain lie,' he said curtly.

'Don't call me a liar.'

'No, but I will call your bluff.' His arm whipped out and he gathered her in, a small fury.

'You want a scandal? Do you really?' She was trembling with rage and frustrated longing.

'There's too much of that in the world,' he responded grimly. 'I'm taking you back, Morgan, so damned well hush. You talk about living a lie? You're living a lie now. You say you don't love me. Let's decide that now.'

A moment later she felt his mouth close over hers and her frenzy increased. She was burning hot, panting and turning her head in a delirium as he covered her face and throat with kisses, returning still more masterfully to her mouth. How terrible was this deep yearning! Soon his hands were caressing her and she could not stay him.

He moved them to the bed, her senses so excited she was moaning from the force.

'This is strange for a girl who doesn't love me,' he muttered. The nipples of her breasts were tight buds pressing against the silk crêpe de Chine of her top, and he lowered his mouth over the soft, thin material.

'Please, Ty.' Her mood was violent and erotic.

There was a flush on his sun-coppered skin. 'You can't trust me, eh? You poor, misguided child. I've been looking after you for years!'

Sensation was dizzying. 'I can't bear to be worsted,' she gasped.

'You're going to be worsted now.' He pulled the simple, elegant white top over her head, his speed and efficiency stunning her. She was still wearing the matching narrow skirt, but it was rucked up so that her beautiful slender legs were on full display. 'What I feel for you, Morgan, is a rare thing. I'm not going to allow your habitual stubbornness to keep us apart.'

She made a sound between rejection and surrender, but then her body was going into spasms as he bent his head to her naked breast. His caresses advanced to the point when her slender legs were thrashing, and only then did he break off his downward conquest, staring into her passion-drugged face. Her every struggle had subsided, her whole being was aflame. Given over to him.

'You seem to have nothing to say,' he taunted her. Not even "stop". If so, please tell me why. You're a virgin, yet you're mine for the taking. Think about it. Am I the enemy, or am I the man you desperately want to marry?'

Truth pushed through her terrible constraints. 'My only concern is you!' she cried. 'Can't you look at it from my side?' Tears filled her huge green eyes.

'But of course I can.' He lowered his head with great tenderness and took a single crystal tear into his mouth. 'I know your feeling of terrible disillusionment goes back a long way. I can't condone what your mother did, but we have to believe she did if for you. Generally, people will do anything for money.'

'I can't take what is not mine.' She stared up at him, appealing for understanding.

'And I cannot take what I believe you have earned. More, my mother is in entire agreement.'

'But only if I marry you?' She flushed.

'Shall we say my mother has always known my feelings for you, Morgan. There's an indestructible bond between us. Yet I still haven't made you say you love me.'

'Nor have you said that to me.' A shadow moved across her lustrous eyes.

'How can you be so bright and so dense?' he demanded. 'I could have told you I loved you when you were about fourteen, but common decency prevented it. I've had to wait for you to reach womanhood. It taught me a lot. Plenty of patience and forbearance. A quirky sense of humour with you weaving and ducking like a little prize fighter. Some of the time I enjoyed it hugely. Other times I came disastrously close to just scooping you up and riding into the bush. Don't tell me you didn't know, deep down in your heart.'

She sighed and briefly closed her eyes. 'I suppose I did. The hostility excited me, too. It was my only defence.'

His hands moved sensuously over the delicate slope of her shoulder, his intention quiet unmistakable. 'So your very considerable "hatred" for me was only a powerfully hidden love?'

'You have your victory.' She arched her body to gain the satisfaction she craved.

'Victory?' He laughed, but not from pure joy. He cupped her face between strong, urgent hands. 'What is this victory you speak of? I won't have you thinking of your admission of love in that way. It's demeaning to you and to me.'

She sighed ruefully. 'It was no great advantage having E.J. rear me. To a very great extent I'm frightened of love.'

'So I'll have to show you,' he said with rich persuasion. 'There's nothing in this world I want more.'

'And I want it too, Ty,' she cried emotionally. 'God, how I want it! But what happens if my story gets out? What happens if the person who hates me sends the follow-up photographs to the newspapers? Can't you just see it? "Hartland Heiress a Fraud."'

'Hush, be still for a moment,' he soothed her. 'You were reared a Hartland. A Hartland you remain. I've already moved to ensure Camilla—who else?—never falls into that error again. Please believe me when I tell you you don't have to worry on that score. The curious thing is that what was only a vague suspicion and a whole lot of spite on her part was so readily apparent to us. She acted mainly out of a desire to shock and upset. She won't try that one again. Not ever. Our marriage will deflect all speculation.'

'Because you love me?'

'In this world and the next.' He bent and kissed her velvety eyelids. 'Let me show you, my darling, so you can understand.'

The engagement between Ty and Morgan was formally announced at Morgan's gala ball. Family, friends, the two hundred guests, burst into spontaneous applause. It was obvious from Morgan's radiance that she was very much in love and feeling deeply cherished. Ty, for his part, projected his happiness and male pride in his bride-to-be.

'So E.J. gets to finish what he started,' Henry murmured to Cecilia. 'In my view, that gives *real* meaning to his life.'

Love is the most valuable possession of all.

INDULGE A LITTLE SWEEPSTAKES

OFFICIAL RULES

SWEEPSTAKES RULES AND REGULATIONS. NO PURCHASE NECESSARY.

1. NO PURCHASE NECESSARY. To enter complete the official entry form and return with the invoice in the envelope provided. Or you may enter by printing your name, complete address and your daytime phone number on a 3 x 5 piece of paper. Include with your entry the hand printed words "Indulge A Little Sweepstakes." Mail your entry to: Indulge A Little Sweepstakes, P.O. Box 1397, Buffalo, NY 14269-1397. No mechanically reproduced entries accepted. Not responsible for late, lost, misdirected mail, or printing errors.

2. Three winners, one per month (Sept. 30, 1989, October 31, 1989 and November 30, 1989), will be selected in random drawings. All entries received prior to the drawing date will be eligible for that month's prize. This sweepstakes is under the supervision of MARDEN-KANE, INC. an independent judging organization whose decisions are final and binding. Winners will be notified by telephone and may be required to execute an affidavit of eligibility and release which must be returned within 14 days, or an alternate winner will be selected.

3. Prizes: 1st Grand Prize (1) a trip for two to Disneyworld in Orlando, Florida. Trip includes round trip air transportation, hotel accommodations for seven days and six nights, plus up to $700 expense money (ARV $3,500). 2nd Grand Prize (1) a seven-night Chandris Caribbean Cruise for two includes transportation from nearest major airport, accommodations, meals plus up to $1,000 in expense money (ARV $4,300). 3rd Grand Prize (1) a ten-day Hawaiian holiday for two includes round trip air transportation for two, hotel accommodations, sightseeing, plus up to $1,200 in spending money (ARV $7,700). All trips subject to availability and must be taken as outlined on the entry form.

4. Sweepstakes open to residents of the U.S. and Canada 18 years or older except employees and the families of Torstar Corp., its affiliates, subsidiaries and Marden-Kane, Inc. and all other agencies and persons connected with conducting this sweepstakes. All Federal, State and local laws and regulations apply. Void wherever prohibited or restricted by law. Taxes, if any are the sole responsibility of the prize winners. Canadian winners will be required to answer a skill testing question. Winners consent to the use of their name, photograph and/or likeness for publicity purposes without additional compensation.

5. For a list of prize winners, send a stamped, self-addressed envelope to Indulge A Little Sweepstakes Winners, P.O. Box 701, Sayreville, NJ 08871.

© 1989 HARLEQUIN ENTERPRISES LTD.

DL-SWPS

INDULGE A LITTLE SWEEPSTAKES

OFFICIAL RULES

SWEEPSTAKES RULES AND REGULATIONS. NO PURCHASE NECESSARY.

1. NO PURCHASE NECESSARY. To enter complete the official entry form and return with the invoice in the envelope provided. Or you may enter by printing your name, complete address and your daytime phone number on a 3 x 5 piece of paper. Include with your entry the hand printed words "Indulge A Little Sweepstakes." Mail your entry to: Indulge A Little Sweepstakes, P.O. Box 1397, Buffalo, NY 14269-1397. No mechanically reproduced entries accepted. Not responsible for late, lost, misdirected mail, or printing errors.

2. Three winners, one per month (Sept. 30, 1989, October 31, 1989 and November 30, 1989), will be selected in random drawings. All entries received prior to the drawing date will be eligible for that month's prize. This sweepstakes is under the supervision of MARDEN-KANE, INC. an independent judging organization whose decisions are final and binding. Winners will be notified by telephone and may be required to execute an affidavit of eligibility and release which must be returned within 14 days, or an alternate winner will be selected.

3. Prizes: 1st Grand Prize (1) a trip for two to Disneyworld in Orlando, Florida. Trip includes round trip air transportation, hotel accommodations for seven days and six nights, plus up to $700 expense money (ARV $3,500). 2nd Grand Prize (1) a seven-night Chandris Caribbean Cruise for two includes transportation from nearest major airport, accommodations, meals plus up to $1,000 in expense money (ARV $4,300). 3rd Grand Prize (1) a ten-day Hawaiian holiday for two includes round trip air transportation for two, hotel accommodations, sightseeing, plus up to $1,200 in spending money (ARV $7,700). All trips subject to availability and must be taken as outlined on the entry form.

4. Sweepstakes open to residents of the U.S. and Canada 18 years or older except employees and the families of Torstar Corp., its affiliates, subsidiaries and Marden-Kane, Inc. and all other agencies and persons connected with conducting this sweepstakes. All Federal, State and local laws and regulations apply. Void wherever prohibited or restricted by law. Taxes, if any are the sole responsibility of the prize winners. Canadian winners will be required to answer a skill testing question. Winners consent to the use of their name, photograph and/or likeness for publicity purposes without additional compensation.

5. For a list of prize winners, send a stamped, self-addressed envelope to Indulge A Little Sweepstakes Winners, P.O. Box 701, Sayreville, NJ 08871.

© 1989 HARLEQUIN ENTERPRISES LTD.

DL-SWPS

INDULGE A LITTLE—WIN A LOT!

Summer of '89 Subscribers-Only Sweepstakes

OFFICIAL ENTRY FORM

This entry must be received by: Sept. 30, 1989
This month's winner will be notified by: October 7, 1989
Trip must be taken between: Nov. 7, 1989–Nov. 7, 1990

YES, I want to win the Walt Disney World® vacation for two! I understand the prize includes round-trip airfare, first-class hotel, and a daily allowance as revealed on the "Wallet" scratch-off card.

Name_____

Address_____

City_____State/Prov._____Zip/Postal Code_____

Daytime phone number_____
                         Area code

Return entries with invoice in envelope provided. Each book in this shipment has two entry coupons—and the more coupons you enter, the better your chances of winning!

© 1989 HARLEQUIN ENTERPRISES LTD.

DINDL-1

INDULGE A LITTLE—WIN A LOT!

Summer of '89 Subscribers-Only Sweepstakes

OFFICIAL ENTRY FORM

This entry must be received by: Sept. 30, 1989
This month's winner will be notified by: October 7, 1989
Trip must be taken between: Nov. 7, 1989–Nov. 7, 1990

YES, I want to win the Walt Disney World® vacation for two! I understand the prize includes round-trip airfare, first-class hotel, and a daily allowance as revealed on the "Wallet" scratch-off card.

Name_____

Address_____

City_____State/Prov._____Zip/Postal Code_____

Daytime phone number_____
                         Area code

Return entries with invoice in envelope provided. Each book in this shipment has two entry coupons—and the more coupons you enter, the better your chances of winning!

© 1989 HARLEQUIN ENTERPRISES LTD.

DINDL-1